CLARE BALDING

The Racehorse Who Disappeared

Illustrated by TONY ROSS

PUFFIN

PUFFIN BOOKS

UK | USA | Canada | Ireland | Australia
India | New Zealand | South Africa

Puffin Books is part of the Penguin Random House group of companies
whose addresses can be found at global.penguinrandomhouse.com.

www.penguin.co.uk   www.puffin.co.uk   www.ladybird.co.uk

Penguin
Random House
UK

First published 2017
This edition published 2018

001

Text copyright © Clare Balding, 2017
Illustrations copyright © Tony Ross, 2017

The moral right of the author and illustrator has been asserted

Set in 12.25/20pt AbsaraOT by Mandy Norman
Printed in Great Britain by Clays Ltd, St Ives plc

A CIP catalogue record for this book is available from the British Library

ISBN: 978-0-141-37738-4

All correspondence to:
Puffin Books
Penguin Random House Children's
80 Strand, London WC2R ORL

For the real Granny Pam,
who says adults are allowed to read this too!

The Folly Farm family

Charlie

Granny Pam

Mr Bass

Mrs Bass

Harry

Larry

Polly

Joe

Chapter 1

Boris stood at the top of the stairs with his head on one side, looking suspiciously at the front door. He was motionless, as if frozen by a magic spell, apart from the gentle twitching of his nose. He had been standing like this for three minutes, ever since he had picked up the distant rumble of a van on the drive. It was a sound no human ear could have detected, but Boris had exceptional hearing. He was a Border terrier with extrasensory perception.

'What's the matter, Boris?'

Charlie tousled his hair and broke the spell. He looked at her, and then again at the door. With a thud, the morning papers landed on the doormat and Boris started barking and ran full pelt down the stairs, three at a time. He landed, still running and barking, on the red stone floor at the bottom, skidded to a halt just before hitting the front door and grabbed a newspaper in his mouth.

Charlie bounded down the stairs behind him and started their morning tug of war with the *Racing Post*. Boris growled and closed his eyes with the effort of hanging on to the paper. Charlie gripped the two ends that were sticking out of the sides of his mouth and lifted him off the ground. She dragged him into the kitchen, where only the offer of a biscuit would convince Boris to relax his jaw and give up the newspaper.

Polly, Charlie's best friend who had come to stay for the weekend, laughed as she followed them down the stairs.

'Why does he want that newspaper so much?' she asked.

'I don't know, but he's done this every day for the last three weeks. I think it's because he saw his photo on the front page the day after the Derby so now he thinks the paper belongs to him,' said Charlie, smiling.

After breakfast, Charlie, Polly and Boris wandered outside to check on the horses. It was a bright, sunny summer's morning on Folly Farm, and the air was full of swifts darting across the farmyard from their nests under the eaves of the big barn. Charlie and Polly leaned on the gate, watching Noble Warrior and Percy relaxing in the field. They were having a little holiday after their exploits at Epsom. Just a couple of weeks of complete rest and relaxation – a 'staycation' for horses.

Charlie's older brothers, Harry and Larry, were feeding the pigs and, once they had dispatched their duties, came over to join them. Charlie could see they wanted something just by the way they were walking. Boris had calmed down and was sniffing the fence, picking exactly the right post on which to cock his leg.

'We need to hold an Open Day for Noble Warrior,' Harry announced. 'All the big stables do it when they've had a Derby winner.' He sounded authoritative, but that didn't mean much. He had been on a self-confidence course at school and now seemed to think that the trick to being successful in life was to sound like an expert, even if he had no idea what he was talking about.

'Do they?' Charlie looked quizzically at her brother.

'Absolutely,' replied Harry, putting on his best Winston Churchill voice. 'It's your duty as the trainer of the Derby winner to parade him in front of his adoring fans. He may be Noddy to us, but he's Noble Warrior to the millions who watched him and read about him. You must open the gates and let the public in!'

'Do you reckon we could make any money out of them?' Larry, who was a year younger than Harry, was suddenly interested. 'Charge them a few quid for tickets and sell them overpriced ice creams?'

'Honestly, Larry,' sighed Charlie. 'You got your share of the prize money for winning the Derby and you've bought all sorts of new stuff: an iPhone, an iPad, an iSpy and iWant – what more is there?'

Charlie was a little disappointed that her brothers had fallen so willingly into the world of 'must-have' gadgets.

'Yeah, but most of the money went on repairing the roof and the rest is being saved to resurface the drive. *Booooring!* What we *really* need is a fully integrated sound system for the farmyard. Music is the beat that makes us move and, if we're ever going to get them to dance properly, they need to hear it.'

'Who's "they"?' asked Charlie.

'The chickens, obviously. Who else? *Strictly Come Chicken Dancing* is the BEST idea in the world and it will be brilliant TV. We just need to teach them to dance, and we can't do that without speakers everywhere and a remote control so I can change the track from salsa to tango and show them how the moves are different.'

Larry put one arm across his body, stretched the other one out to the right and started to move, as if dancing with an imaginary partner. He flicked his head from side to side and raised one leg, bending it at the knee. He had such a severe expression on his face that Charlie couldn't help but burst out laughing. He glared at her.

'I'm serious. This could be the key to our long-term fortune. No choreographer in history has successfully taught chickens to tango. But if I'm going to be the first, I need a sound system and, to pay for that, Noddy has to win another big race – like the King George or the Arc de Triomphe in Paris. Now there's a city that would appreciate dancing chickens. They've got style and culture, those Parisians.'

'Why don't we wait until then to have the Open Day?' Charlie asked. 'The Arc isn't until October and it feels better to celebrate at the end of the season rather than halfway through.'

'It'll be muddy by then,' said Harry, taking charge again. 'We'd ruin the fields if we parked cars in there in the autumn. It's got to be now, while it's fresh in everyone's minds.'

Charlie hadn't been prepared for all the attention that had come her way after winning the Derby. She was the first female – and by far the youngest person – ever to train the winner. She and Joe Butler, the farmhand who helped her father milk the cows, had transformed Noble Warrior from a nervous, reluctant jelly who refused to race into a world-beater. The family had been offered millions of pounds for him, but he was not for sale, not at any price.

Oh, and then there was Percy. The fat, grumpy, hairy little pony without whom Noble Warrior couldn't function. Percy had played his part too, carrying Charlie across the middle of the Epsom Downs to get to the winning post before the runners reached it. He wasn't for sale either, not that anyone had offered.

When Noble Warrior had seen his friend Percy ahead of him, just beyond the finish, he had thundered down the straight so fast that Joe said it was like flying. In the photo finish, Noble Warrior's black nose had just nudged ahead at the line. From the racehorse who wouldn't gallop to the racehorse who won the Derby, Noddy had done them proud. They had made history.

But ever since then, one big question had been swimming around Charlie's head. The question that anyone who has achieved their dream asks themselves the very next day: *What next? What should be my goal now and how will I achieve it?*

'Have you thought about trying anything else with him?' Polly was chewing on a long, sweet stem of grass as she watched Noble Warrior roll, scratching his back on the sun-baked ground and wiggling his legs in the air. Boris mirrored his actions by rolling on the edge of the muck heap. He got up and shook himself, sniffed his back and wagged his tail, clearly pleased with his new aroma.

Polly was the reason the Bass family had bought Noble Warrior in the first place. Charlie had been at a horse auction, waving to get her friend's attention. Unfortunately, the auctioneer took her

wave as the first and only bid on Noble Warrior, and so her father ended up paying a thousand pounds for a racehorse they didn't want and couldn't afford. But Polly and her parents had pitched in to help. Polly's dad, Alex Williams, was a bona fide racehorse trainer, and he had allowed Charlie to train Noble Warrior on his gallops at Cherrydown Stables. Without the Williams's generosity, there was no way Noddy could have won the Derby.

'Trying something else? What do you mean?' Charlie was always open to new ideas, particularly if they came from Polly rather than her idiot brothers.

'Well, some really famous horses have become celebrities in their own right,' Polly explained. 'Red Rum turned on the Blackpool Illuminations one year. Desert Orchid used to open supermarkets. And apparently Frankel does on-demand selfies! Dad sometimes sends a horse off to learn another sport. A really small racehorse might do better as a polo pony, or one that's too slow for racing might be suitable for showjumping or eventing.

Racehorses can switch to endurance riding and team chasing, and even sports like polocrosse and horseball.'

'What're they?' asked Harry.

'Ball sports that you play on horseback,' Polly explained. 'You have to have a brilliant horse, because most of the time you can't use your reins to steer them because you're too busy catching or throwing a ball. It can be quite dangerous.'

'Epic!' gasped Larry.

Charlie watched Noble Warrior heaving himself to his feet. 'Hmm. It's an interesting idea, but he's only just got the hang of being a racehorse. I don't fancy trying to teach him not to be scared of a ball flying through the air!'

'I hadn't thought of that,' laughed Polly. 'He'd probably think it was a spaceship come to attack him. Poor old Noddy, he's always scared of what might happen and he doesn't know how lucky he is to live in the safest place on earth.'

Noble Warrior walked languidly towards them and put his head over the gate.

'I know,' said Charlie, stroking his head. 'His only worry is whether or not he can finish his food before Percy butts in!'

'That's another reason we should have an Open Day,' said Harry. 'To give Noddy a chance to get used to big crowds again. If we do it here at home, he'll be fine when he gets to Ascot or Longchamp.'

'OK,' said Charlie, pulling Noble Warrior's ear gently and speaking into it. 'If it will help you in the long run, I suppose we can do it.'

'Excellent!' Harry clapped his hands, making Noble Warrior jump backwards. Harry carried on, oblivious. 'I was thinking the first of July. It's a Sunday and, if we do it then, we've still got four weeks to get him ready for the King George.'

'The first of July? But that's only a week away!' Charlie was horrified. 'How are we going to be ready in time? And how will people even know it's happening?'

'Ah, don't worry about that,' muttered Larry, tapping on his phone. 'It only takes a second to tell the world something big is coming . . .'

He held the phone up in front of Charlie and Noble Warrior and took a photo.

'There we go. "Just chillin': Derby winner on holiday with his trainer. Come and see them for yourselves. 1 July. Folly Farm. Tickets only £10. #selfieop #champion." Perfect!'

'Ten pounds?' exclaimed Charlie. 'Larry, that's too much.'

'All right, all right, Bossy Pants. I'll make it two.' He started tapping again. "Tickets only £2 per person, £5 for the whole family. #bargain #toocheap #grabitquick." There: sent.'

'So who's going to see that?' asked Charlie.

'Only everyone on Twitter, Instagram, Snapchat and Facebook. Plus the twenty thousand people who've subscribed to my YouTube channel since we won the Derby.' He looked down at his phone as it started pinging. 'Yup, thought as much. Looks like the fans will be flocking here on the first of July. Oh, yeah!' Larry high-fived Harry, then grabbed his brother in an embrace and tangoed him towards the house.

'C'mon, bro, we've got chickens to train,' said Harry.

'And money to drain,' replied Larry, as they shimmied away.

Charlie sighed and looked despairingly at Polly. 'You're so lucky not to have brothers,' she said, leaning down to stroke Boris. 'They always think they know best and then just go ahead and do things, whether I want to or not.'

Polly shrugged her shoulders.

'Technically, they did wait until you said yes about the Open Day, but I know what you mean.'

'They don't understand how much there'll be to organize, and I bet it'll end up being me that has to do it all. They'll be off with their stupid chickens. I just want to make sure Noddy doesn't get scared and that Percy doesn't try to bite anyone. You will help me, won't you?'

Polly reached out and patted Charlie's arm.

'Of course I will. That's what best friends are for.'

'Thanks, Polly!' Charlie lifted her hand and

sniffed it. 'Oh, no! What's he been rolling in now? Boris, you little monster, you stink!'

Boris looked up at his owner and wagged his tail. He grinned at her and then started spinning round on the spot. Charlie and Polly laughed. They couldn't help it. Even when he did something awful, Boris got away with it because he was funny.

'Hey, girls! How's tricks?' Joe was walking towards them, two ropes in his hand. 'It's time to get this pair back indoors. The forecast says it's going to rain later and we don't want them getting wet and catching a cold.'

Polly looked down at her shoes.

'Here you go.' Joe passed Charlie one of the ropes. 'You take Percy, but be careful he doesn't drag you across the field. He knows it's nearly lunchtime. Polly, do you want to take Noddy?'

Polly took the rope without looking at Joe and nodded her head.

'You're very quiet, Polly,' said Charlie. 'What's the matter?'

'Nothing,' muttered Polly, shaking her head

vigorously and scuttling into the field to click the rope on to Noble Warrior's headcollar.

Joe led the way, with Charlie and Polly behind him, while Boris half trotted, half hopped along beside them, alternately lifting one back leg and then the other.

'So I hear we're having an Open Day in a couple of weeks,' said Joe. 'The boys told me this morning. They want me to come in my racing breeches and colours. I said it might look a bit daft away from the racecourse, but –'

'Hang on,' Charlie interrupted. 'They told you this morning?'

'Yes, before breakfast. Harry said they were just clearing up a few minor details before they announced it. Larry mentioned it on Facebook yesterday in a very cryptic way. "Want to meet a Derby winner? Big announcement coming soon."'

'He wrote that *yesterday*? They only asked me just now!' Charlie shook her head in disbelief and, as she slackened the rope, Percy seized the opportunity to get free. He charged towards the barn, pushing past Noble Warrior.

'Ow!' cried Charlie when the rope started to burn as Percy pulled it through her hands.

'Let go!' shouted Joe. 'Just drop the rope!'

Charlie was pulled forward with such force that she fell on to her stomach and was dragged over the cobbles. Still she tried to cling on.

'Let go!' Joe shouted again. 'I mean it – let go before you get hurt!'

Charlie finally heeded his advice. Percy cantered free towards the barn, where he buried his head in Noble Warrior's bucket of feed. Joe helped Charlie to her feet while Polly led Noble Warrior gently towards the barn.

'Noddy, you're a good boy, aren't you? You wouldn't be that rude,' Polly said, as she unclipped his rope and shut the gate behind them both. 'I think you'd apologize for him if you could.'

Noble Warrior looked at Percy, who was gobbling as fast as he could, and then back at Polly. He lowered his nose and nuzzled her neck.

Charlie dusted off her legs and examined her hands.

'You'll need a bit of ice on those palms,' Joe said. 'Polly, will you take her in and look after her? I just need to make sure Percy hasn't eaten all the protein mix, the little blighter.'

Back in the kitchen, Charlie held her hands under the cold tap. Her palms were red and sore.

'I'll get you some ice in a tea towel and you can hold that for a while. It'll help stimulate the blood flow. We do it with the racehorses all the time,' said Polly.

'It'll be fine in a minute,' Charlie replied. 'I'm just cross with myself that I lost concentration and let him take advantage. When food is involved, Percy will do anything to get to it.'

'Do you want me to look after him during the Open Day?' Polly offered. 'That way you can relax and just focus on Noddy. I won't get distracted and I'll make sure I wear gloves in case he tries to do the same to me.'

'Would you do that?' Charlie never failed to be impressed by her friend's thoughtfulness. 'That would be really kind. It wouldn't be great if he got loose and suddenly rampaged through the crowds in search of an ice cream.'

Polly nodded her agreement.

'Thanks, Polly. You're the best!'

Chapter 2

Charlie couldn't believe so many people had turned up. There were dozens of cars parked in the field and more snaking down the drive. Larry was in charge of parking and, looking from the kitchen window at the crooked lines of vehicles, Charlie now regretted that delegation decision. She hoped her brother would politely prevent the visitors from coming into the farmyard until the proper time.

For the past five days, her brothers had been trying to teach the chickens to form a guard of honour, but it hadn't worked. If they couldn't get them to perform a simple obedience test like that, what hope did they ever have of teaching them to tango? Their dreams of a TV series of *Strictly Come Chicken Dancing* were crushed. Luckily, they'd got over the disappointment already and had moved on to the pigs, Elvis and Doris, whom Harry was convinced could be living, breathing metal detectors if they were trained correctly.

'There's this pig in Italy,' he said from his place at the breakfast table. 'She's called Mona Lisa and she's sniffed out ten thousand pounds' worth of truffles. I mean, how cool is that? Talk about bringing home the bacon before *becoming* the bacon!'

Harry had taken a sip of tea, but he was laughing so hard at his own joke that he had to spit it out before he snorted it out of his nose.

'That's gross!' said Charlie, as she pushed her chair back and left the kitchen.

Her breakfast conversations with her brothers nearly always ended like this. It was as if they saw the line between appropriate and inappropriate and took a running jump at it to make sure they landed on the far side.

'It's all a game to the boys,' said Charlie's mum, Caroline, following her into the hall. 'They think of things to say that will annoy or upset you and, my darling, you fall for it every time. You're going to have to learn not to rise to the bait because it only encourages them.'

She reached out to Charlie and pulled her close.

'My little warrior. I know you look for the best in everyone, but I fear your brothers are beyond redemption. You'll have to do your own thing and there's no point having dreams unless they're big ones – after all, it was you who dreamed we could win the Derby and you got that one right. The bank would have taken the farm if it wasn't for you.'

Charlie's face was buried in her mother's jumper so her reply was a bit muffled.

"Snot me you should fank. It was Noggy and Go who did it.'

'What?' Her mother released Charlie to let her breathe and speak clearly.

'It's not me you should thank,' she repeated. 'It was Noddy and Joe who did it.'

'Ah, but we all know that without you and Percy it would never have happened.'

She gave her daughter one last hug.

'Right, you need to make sure the yard is looking spick and span and I need to check on my gingerbread and mashed-potato cake.'

'Are you sure it was meant to have mashed potato in it?' Charlie queried. Her mother read books for a living, but her ability to follow a recipe accurately had never been a strength.

'Well, it was meant to be grated carrots with the gingerbread, but we've given them all to Percy and Noddy, so I've used potatoes instead. We had a spare bag and I honestly don't think anyone will notice.'

Charlie wasn't so sure. She made a mental note

not to eat any of the snacks on offer. By the looks of the crowds arriving, they wouldn't have enough anyway, so she'd better warn the rest of the gang that it was a case of FHB: Family Hold Back.

Suddenly Boris started barking. A minute later, Charlie heard a car screeching to a halt outside. She ran to open the front door. Behind the wheel of a dark green convertible was a woman wearing a headscarf, large sunglasses and bright red lipstick.

'Darling!' she shouted, as she switched off the engine and violently pulled the handbrake up. 'I'm so sorry I'm late. Got stuck behind a tractor. Crawling it was, no faster than a snail. So FRUSTRATING!'

'Granny Pam!' cried Charlie. 'You came!'

Granny Pam was Caroline's mother and she was always late. She would say it was the traffic or sheep in the road or a sudden eclipse, but Charlie suspected it was because she always left home half an hour later than she should have done.

'Never mind, I'm HERE NOW!' Granny Pam swung her legs out of the driver's seat and slammed

the door behind her. She glided towards Charlie and kissed her on both cheeks, making a lot of noise but no contact with her face.

Granny Pam had been an actress in her youth and still maintained something of a dramatic nature. She was always immaculately dressed and wouldn't be seen dead without her hair and make-up in place. She was also slightly deaf, which may have been why she sometimes spoke VERY LOUDLY, as if she was still on stage. Projecting, she called it.

'We're going to put on such a SHOW this weekend,' she said, as she sailed into the house. 'This will be the Open Day to end all Open Days. We'll give it a touch of the business of show. We need to make an entrance, shake a leg, create a little razzamatazz. THEATRE! That's what it needs.'

Granny Pam pronounced 'theatre' as if it was three separate words – THEE-AH-TER. She gestured with her arms like a dancer. 'But first I require TEA!' she proclaimed. 'That journey always leaves me parched!'

'Come into the kitchen then, Mum,' said Caroline, looking slightly flustered as she always did when her mother visited. 'There's a pot on the go. Charlie has things to do, don't you, love?'

Charlie nodded. 'See you later, Granny Pam.'

Charlie and Polly headed out into the yard. They fed the horses, the pigs and the chickens, and collected the eggs. Then they swept the yard and hosed it down, and took a cup of tea to Charlie's dad, who was hosing down the milking shed.

When she had the chance, Charlie ran upstairs to

change, leaving Polly to help Mrs Bass in the kitchen. She rummaged around for a pair of jeans that weren't covered in mud and slipped on the jacket she had been given when Noble Warrior ran in the Derby. Granny Pam had added a bit of creative needlework to the back so that instead of saying **Noble Warrior, Derby Runner** it now read **Noble Warrior, Derby Winner**.

'Hey, Boris,' she said. 'You need a new outfit as well. There we go – that looks splendid!'

Charlie stepped back to admire his new red-and-white spotted neckerchief. It set off his dark brown eyes and gave him a country cowboy swagger. Boris sat with his head on one side, not sure if the new addition was quite him, and let out a quizzical squeak.

'Come on, boy, let's get this show on the road,' said Charlie.

Boris jumped up and barked his approval before slipping past her and galloping down the stairs. He turned a circle at the bottom, and then another, growling at his tail as if he'd forgotten it was actually part of his own body.

'You are a daft dog,' laughed Charlie at her beloved Border terrier.

'Charlie, can you give this letter to Joe?' asked Caroline. 'It arrived this morning.'

'Will do,' replied Charlie, glancing at the postmark. 'Looks like it's from Ireland. I didn't realize Joe knew anyone out there.'

'Maybe it's one of his dad's old jockey friends,' said Polly. 'I'll catch you up in a minute. I'm just helping put the icing on your mum's rhubarb and radish scones.'

Boris ran across the farmyard towards Joe, who was busy grooming Noble Warrior, making sure he looked the part for his parade. Boris jumped up at Joe, who leaned down to scratch his ears. Boris squirmed with pleasure and rolled on to his back.

'Ooh, that's good, isn't it, Boris?' said Joe. 'I know, yes, I do. I know. The best things in life are food, sleep and having a good tummy rub.'

Joe smiled up at Charlie. 'Sometimes I wish I could be just like Boris,' he said. 'Not worry about anything, be happy just to be me and make the most of every day.'

Charlie looked at Boris, who was now digging himself a nest in the straw. Percy shot him a warning glance with his ears back, to make sure he stayed away from the hay he was munching.

'It's true,' she said. 'Noddy has his insecurity and Percy has his greed, but, apart from his tendency to wear manure as aftershave, Boris is pretty perfect.'

Joe had finished plaiting Noble Warrior's mane and now started brushing him with a body brush, wiping him with a soft, brushed-cotton stable rubber after every stroke. Soon his body was gleaming like polished ebony. He was a beautiful animal. Strong and muscular, yet sleek and toned.

Joe moved on to brushing his tail, which flowed behind him like fine strands of cotton. Noddy was almost jet-black with no white markings on him at all. Percy, on the other hand, had nabbed all the colours in the paintbox. He had one blue eye and one pale brown, a golden body and a creamy white mane and tail. He had a pink nose and a broad white stripe down the centre of his face.

'Beauty and the Beast,' said Joe, as he looked from one to the other.

'Shhh!' Charlie put her hands over Percy's ears. 'He'll hear you and you don't want to get on the wrong side of him. He still hasn't forgiven Harry for calling him U-G-L-Y when he first saw him.' Percy had nearly broken Harry's foot that day and Charlie was convinced it was because he could understand certain words in English. She'd tried grooming him as best she could, but, no matter how hard she tried to make his mane lie flat, it would always pop up again into a messy Mohican.

'Oh, by the way, this came for you,' said Charlie, remembering the letter.

'Can you read it to me?' said Joe. 'I've got my hands full at the moment.'

Charlie carefully opened the envelope.

'It's from Seamus O'Reilly, the Irish trainer!' she exclaimed. 'He was so nice to me on Derby Day, even though we beat all his horses.'

'Why's he writing to me?' asked Joe.

'Let's find out. "Dear Joe,"' Charlie read. '"I hope you'll remember that we met briefly on Derby Day" –'

'Remember?' Joe interrupted. 'He's the champion trainer. He's my hero. Of course I remember meeting him!'

'Maybe he's just being modest,' explained Charlie, 'and doesn't want to assume that you'll only remember him because he's famous. Anyway, listen to what he's got to say.'

She continued reading.

'"I was very impressed with your riding that day. In fact, it was more than just that, it was your horsemanship that I noticed. Many jockeys can ride a fast finish and plenty are good judges of pace, but not everyone is a natural horseman as well. You have a very special gift, Joe, and I wanted to ask if you might be interested in working for me" –'

Charlie stopped suddenly and looked at Joe, her mouth dropping open.

'Here,' said Joe. 'Give it to me.'

He quickly read the rest of the letter while

Charlie practically skipped on the spot. For Joe, who wanted to have a career as a jockey, this was the chance of a lifetime.

'Gosh,' Joe said when he had finished the letter. 'He says that he knows I'll always want to ride Noble Warrior and he'd let me do that, even if he has a runner in the same race, but that he'd love me to be a part of his team.'

'Joe, that's fantastic!' Charlie exclaimed. 'He's the best trainer in Europe, probably in the world, and now he wants you to ride his horses! It's amazing!'

Charlie beamed up at Joe, expecting him to be grinning back at her. But his face was serious, sad even.

'What's the matter, Joe?' she asked. 'This is *good* news, isn't it?'

Joe swallowed and answered slowly.

'It's great news. It's what I've always dreamed of. But there's a problem. A big problem.'

'What do you mean?' asked Charlie, confused.

'Charlie, he wants me to move to Ireland.'

Chapter 3

'Oh.'

Charlie finally understood. This was one of the biggest jobs in racing. Of course Joe couldn't do it from a farm in the middle of nowhere. Of course he couldn't milk cows in the morning and ride at Royal Ascot in the afternoon. That would be impossible.

'What are you going to do,' she asked in a small voice.

'I don't know,' Joe replied. 'I mean, I want to be a jockey and win races, but . . . how can I leave Folly Farm? Your family has given me everything.'

Charlie's head was swimming. This was a huge decision for Joe. She didn't want him to leave, but she didn't want to stand in his way either. This was his big break, his opportunity to ride the best horses in the world rather than just one. But she couldn't imagine what the farm would be like without him.

Joe looked at his watch.

'Well, I can't think about it now. It's almost time for the parade.'

'OK,' said Charlie. 'Let's talk about it afterwards. I've told Larry to hit the music at ten thirty exactly and we'll make our entrance.'

Mr Bass came into the barn in his overalls and cap.

'You wouldn't believe how many people have turned up,' he said. 'Hundreds! They're all out there in the yard, drinking fresh milk and eating your mother's cakes.'

Charlie looked surprised.

'I know! They must be hungry!' Bill Bass let out a deep, warm laugh, full of love and appreciation for their good luck.

'Polly's talking to her parents,' he said. 'They've brought some of the staff from Cherrydown and a couple of owners who wanted to see the Derby winner. Most of your teachers from school are here and I think all of your year too. The butcher is chatting to the landlord from The Swan. Granny Pam is talking to everyone and I'm a bit worried as to what on earth she's saying. It's quite a crowd.'

Joe smiled and stroked Noble Warrior's neck.

'All for you, boy. They're all here for you.' Charlie noticed the look of complete adoration in his eyes. Joe loved Noble Warrior so much. No wonder he was in a pickle about whether to accept Seamus O'Reilly's offer.

'Are you getting changed, Dad?' asked Charlie.

'Nah,' Bill Bass replied. 'I got a terrible rash from that tweed suit I was going to wear at Epsom and I feel a lot more at home in overalls. Given that we *are* at home, I think I'd better stick with what makes me comfortable.'

Charlie grinned at him. She loved her dad and his refusal to be swayed by the expectations of other people. When they won a million pounds from the Derby, he said all he wanted were a few things for the farm. No new car or cashmere jumper, no meals in fancy restaurants or expensive holidays. Just a second-hand tractor called Eric and four more cows that they named Jenny, Venetia, Sue and Lucinda after the four women who had trained Grand National winners.

'Are Harry and Larry keeping the crowds entertained?' asked Charlie.

'Well,' said her dad, 'in a way. They've set up a game with the pancakes your mother made. Seems they're a bit on the tough side, so the boys are turning that into an advantage and seeing who can throw their pancake the furthest. It's like the discus competition at the Olympics, only the winner gets a carton of eggs rather than a gold medal. The cameras are loving it.'

'The cameras?'

'Yes,' said Bill. 'Harry and Larry invited loads of TV and radio reporters. There are a few of them here, including a crew from the BBC who are talking about making a documentary. Maybe we'll all end up as famous as Noddy.'

Charlie shrugged. There were girls at school who always talked about wanting to be famous, but she didn't care for the idea at all. She had only agreed to this Open Day because she thought it might be good for Noddy's confidence, not because she wanted to be admired by a crowd of strangers.

As they were chatting, Joe and Charlie put the finishing touches to their charges. The plan was to lead Noble Warrior and Percy into the farmyard where Charlie would make a short speech. Then people would be allowed to take personal photographs with the Derby winner.

'Are you ready?'

Polly had appeared, gloves on and ready to lead Percy. Charlie looked at her watch. It was 10.29 a.m. She sighed.

'Oh, well. If we're going to do it, I suppose we'd

better try and do it properly. Let's go.'

Joe peeled off his overalls to reveal his sparkling clean racing kit. The green-and-gold colours shimmered as he moved. Polly giggled nervously. Joe reached into his bag for his crash hat, covered by the gold cap, and put it on his head.

'I feel a bit of an idiot in this get-up when I'm not riding in a race,' he said.

'You shouldn't. You look very smart,' said Polly quietly. So quietly that Charlie wasn't even sure Joe had heard her.

Suddenly the sound of 'We are the Champions' by Queen came belting out of the portable speakers Larry had ordered from eBay and set up in the yard. The chickens, who had been happily pecking round the cobbles, suddenly scattered, clucking frantically. Those dance lessons from the boys had clearly scarred them for life.

The crowd started clapping as Boris trotted out with Charlie, ahead of Percy led by Polly, and Noble Warrior led by Joe. They walked in a circle and then came to a stop in the middle of the yard.

Hundreds of phones were held up to take photos and videos.

'I'd like to thank you all for coming!' shouted Charlie before Larry ran up to her with a microphone. Suddenly her voice was coming out of the speakers. Noble Warrior raised his head and pricked his ears as Joe stroked his neck to soothe him.

'It really is lovely to see so many people who helped to make our dream come true,' continued Charlie. 'From Mr and Mrs Williams, who let us use their gallops and their horsebox; to Mr Dawson, who gave us the high-protein racehorse feed we needed; Eugene the farrier, who shod Noble Warrior before the Derby; my parents and brothers for being so supportive; and Joe for riding such a brilliant race. But most of all, ladies and gentlemen, today is a celebration of our equine heroes, so three cheers, please, for Percy and for Noble Warrior! Hip hip . . .'

The crowd roared back: 'HOORAY!'

*

The next hour was taken up with letting people take selfies with Noddy and answering questions from all of the children in the local area, most of whom wanted to know more about Percy. Noble Warrior was beautifully relaxed and responded kindly to the children, reaching down and gently nuzzling them. He pricked his ears as the cameras and iPhones clicked constantly but didn't startle or shy away. Charlie smiled with relief. Maybe the Open Day was good for his confidence.

Bill took various groups to meet the cows, who all seemed very pleased to have some attention – apart from Madonna and Princess Anne, who looked even grumpier than usual. Harry was selling eggs at an inflated price and Larry was playing up to the TV cameras by giving them a long and serious lecture about the difficulties of training chickens to dance and the detective abilities of pigs. Meanwhile, much to their surprise, visitors to the milking shed found Granny Pam giving a full-volume rendition of Alan Bennett's *A Woman of No Importance*. Some stayed out of politeness while others shuffled quickly away again.

Boris stuck close to Charlie's side. He wagged his tail at the children and kept his eyes peeled in case they dropped any ice cream, swooping in quickly to mop up the mess. Charlie was just about to slip away for a well-earned break when another group of people cornered her to ask questions about how fast Noble Warrior could gallop and whether Percy had really tried to bite the Queen.

'Is it true that the horse won't go anywhere without the fat – sorry, I mean fit – pony?' asked a man wearing dark glasses and a flat cap. It was hard to see his features, apart from a long, thin mouth, and his voice was barely above a whisper.

Boris started growling and Charlie reached down to pat him, telling him not to worry.

'Well, he's getting better,' she said to the whispering man. 'He'll come out of the barn on his own now, and into the farmyard, but he doesn't like to go any further than that without Percy. They're best friends, you see.'

'Just like us,' said the man next to him, with a

chuckle. He was wearing a black baseball cap pulled low over his eyes. It had a picture of an eagle above a badge with three wide swords, one above the other, on a red background. The man had a loud, jolly voice and a rosy face and he was grinning as he spoke. 'That pony must be somethin' special. What did you give 'im as a reward? I mean, what's 'is favourite food?'

Boris growled again and Charlie tapped him on the nose.

'Stop it, Boris,' she hissed. 'They're just asking questions like everyone else.'

She patted Percy, who looked thrilled that he was getting so much attention.

'Bananas,' she said. 'He loves bananas. We started getting them to help Noble Warrior recover his potassium levels after exercise, but Percy went nuts that he wasn't having any, so we had to give him some as well. Now Noble Warrior spits them out and Percy eats the lot. He loves them more than carrots or mints or sugar lumps. He'd do anything for a banana.'

Percy frisked her pockets in the vain hope of the banana he'd heard mentioned.

'So interesting,' said the whispering man. 'And has Noble Warrior ever tried pulling anything? I mean, a cart or something like that? Me and my friend, we love those old Roman films where they're doing the chariot racing. It's dead exciting.'

Charlie laughed.

'No, we haven't tried anything like that. I think he might be a bit too fragile to risk in a chariot race!'

The whispering man stretched his mouth into a

thin-lipped smile. He looked as if he was about to ask something else, but just then Charlie saw Mr Williams coming over and, when she looked round, the whispering man and his friend had melted back into the crowd.

Boris growled again.

'I don't think he liked them much,' said Polly, as she gripped Percy's rope tightly. 'Can't say I blame him. They were weird.'

'They're probably just gamblers on the lookout for some inside info,' said Joe. 'There are some strange types in racing, believe me.'

He smiled at Polly, who flushed and looked away.

Charlie shook her head. Why was her friend behaving so oddly?

'Charlie!' Harry shouted from the other side of the farmyard. 'We need you over here!'

Leaving Joe and Polly to deal with the selfie-hunters, Charlie walked over to her brother, who was with one of the camera crews.

'This is Dan and Kate from the BBC,' he said,

sounding like Winston Churchill again. 'They're making a documentary about us winning the Derby and they want to talk to you.'

Charlie narrowed her eyes.

'You didn't say anything about me having to give an interview.'

Harry carried on as if she hadn't spoken.

'I've told them all about how Larry and I contributed to Noddy's preparation and, of course, how we were indispensible on the day. For some reason, they still want to talk to you, though.'

Harry shrugged his shoulders as Kate stepped forward to shake Charlie's hand.

'Nice to meet you, Charlie. I'm the producer and we're hoping to make a one-hour documentary about you all. We're calling it *Derby Dreams*. Dan here is the cameraman and we've got some lovely shots today. We just need a few interviews to round things off and then we'll come back another day to watch Noble Warrior in training. Harry said that would be fine.'

'Oh, really?' said Charlie.

Kate didn't pick up on the sarcasm in Charlie's voice or the death stare she shot her brother, and continued enthusiastically. 'Yes, and we were *very* interested in what Harry told us about how Noble Warrior really didn't trust anyone apart from Percy, and how Harry managed to tame the pony's wilder nature so that he could help rather than hinder the racing side of things.'

'He told you that, did he?' Charlie was incredulous at how her brother could rewrite history so shamelessly. 'Yes, well, I think you'd better ask me a few questions then. That is, if you want an accurate account of what *actually* happened . . .'

Chapter 4

'Well, I think that all went swimmingly,' said Mrs Bass, as she poured a cup of tea from the pot. 'So many lovely people came along and they were all so keen to get their photo with Noble Warrior, weren't they, Charlie? They loved that. Who would have thought so many people knew we'd won the Derby? It's amazing.'

'Even more people will know all about it soon,' said Larry. 'That crew who are making the documentary were so impressed with how many people turned up, they want Charlie to go on the *BBC Breakfast* show tomorrow morning to talk about it. Mum and Dad, they want you there too, and Joe, of course. I told them the Open Day was mine and Harry's idea, but they said they didn't need us, which, frankly, was a bit disappointing.'

Larry shook his head. 'They said something about already having a boy band on the sofa so they wanted to balance things out.'

'Can't have too many handsome young men in one show!' said Harry triumphantly. 'That'll be the reason, I guarantee you.'

'They want us on breakfast television?' said Mrs Bass in horror. 'I can't spare a whole day to go up to London and back. I've got books to read and chores to do. Anyway, I've got nothing to wear.'

'Don't worry,' explained Larry. 'It's not in London. It's in Salford. That's not far.'

'Do you know where Salford is?' Mrs Bass didn't trust Larry's geographical knowledge.

'Yeah, it's Devon, isn't it? We went there once on holiday.'

'That's Salcombe, you idiot. Salford is near Manchester. It's hours away.'

'Ohhh,' said Larry, as if something was suddenly making sense in his brain. '*That's* why they kept saying they'd put you up in a hotel tonight.'

'We can't go all the way to Salford,' said Mrs Bass. 'It's out of the question.'

'Darling! You can and you MUST!' Granny Pam waved her arms dramatically. 'I talked to that lovely, sweet girl Kate and I told her you've been a natural performer since you were a toddler. That gorgeous man Dan came to film me in the milking shed and he told me he had NEVER seen Alan Bennett performed quite like it in all his life.'

'I'm sure he hadn't,' Caroline muttered.

'Anyway, they will look after you beautifully and you will SHINE. I'll help you pick something to wear and they'll have a proper make-up artist do your face, darling.'

Mrs Bass frowned.

'Not that you need it,' Granny Pam added hurriedly when she saw Caroline's reaction. 'It's just that the TV lights can be a bit HARSH so they need to put on extra powder.'

'They've even offered to send a car for you,' added Harry. 'I bet it'll be a really posh one. It's coming this evening at six, so as soon as Dad's finished the milking, you can be off to Salford.'

'What's that?' Bill Bass looked up from his magazine; he had been reading about a dairy cow called a Norwegian Red that could produce up to ten thousand litres of rich, creamy milk per year. 'Where are we sailing? I'd quite like to go to Norway if that's an option.'

'Not *sailing*, Dad,' Charlie said slowly. 'Salford. They want us to go on the breakfast show tomorrow morning on the BBC. The boys can stay here with Granny Pam. That's OK with you, Granny, isn't it?'

'What did you say, dear?' Granny Pam was fiddling behind her right ear. 'I'll just switch this hearing aid back on. Had to turn it off with all that applause for my performance in the milking shed.

There we are – now I can hear you again. What was it?'

'Would you mind staying here tonight with the boys?' asked Charlie gently. 'So Mum and Dad and me and Joe can go up to Salford to be on the telly first thing in the morning?'

'Of course, dear,' replied Granny Pam. 'How could I deprive you of your screen debut? Leave the boys here with me. Everything will be FINE.'

At six o'clock precisely, a silver Mercedes made its way carefully up the drive to pick up Bill, Caroline, Joe and Charlie. Boris wanted to come too, but Charlie was worried he might be sick in the car and she wasn't sure if the hotel was dog friendly or not.

'You stay here and look after the boys and Granny Pam,' she said, as she kissed him on the nose. 'Make sure they don't kill each other.'

'Don't stay up too late, boys!' shouted Caroline, as the chauffeur held open the car door for her.

'We won't!' chorused Harry and Larry, smiling innocently.

Charlie shook her head. She knew what those expressions meant. Granny Pam would have her hands full for sure.

'You'll need to avoid a few potholes, I'm afraid,' Mrs Bass explained apologetically to the chauffeur. 'We're getting the drive resurfaced next week.'

'Don't worry, ma'am. I'll take it slowly.'

Even though there were four of them in the car, Charlie was amazed at how much space there was. Her father sat in the front seat while she, her mother and Joe were comfortable in the back. They headed down the drive and turned left into the lane, negotiating roads that grew ever wider and busier before they hit the motorway to take them north.

Charlie was not relishing the prospect of a television interview. She hadn't minded the attention after Noble Warrior won the Derby because it was mostly about him and Percy. But she didn't like it when the attention was solely on her. At least she had Joe to share it with now and it was good for him to get the acclaim for his riding.

Maybe, if he saw Joe on television, Seamus O'Reilly would still let him ride his horses, even if he didn't relocate to Ireland.

Charlie wondered what Harry and Larry were up to back at the farm. She felt a slight twinge of anxiety, but pushed it to the back of her mind. The Open Day had gone really well and that was largely down to the boys, while Granny Pam had more than played her part. Charlie felt a sudden wave of tiredness and closed her eyes. Before long, she was fast asleep in the back of the car as it glided smoothly northwards.

'Right, boys, it's eleven o'clock – time for BED!' announced Granny Pam, fiddling with her hearing aid. 'I'm going to take this out so I can get a good night's sleep. I'm EXHAUSTED from all that excitement today.'

'Us too,' said Larry, yawning loudly. 'We'll be right behind you. Just got to let Boris out for a pee.'

'Oh, you ARE good lads. Always thinking of the animals. Sleep well and I'll see you in the morning.'

Granny Pam smiled indulgently at her grandsons as she closed the door.

Larry turned to Harry and grinned. 'Time for one more DVD, I reckon.'

'Yeah,' Harry replied. 'What about *Aliens vs Vampires*? Mum never lets us watch anything scary like that.'

'Cool!' agreed Larry. 'And Granny Pam won't hear a thing, so it's not as if we'll keep her awake.'

An hour into the film, just as the lead character was about to be eaten by an alien after being bitten by a vampire, Boris whined and pricked up his ears. He ran to the door and growled, before scampering back to the television, barking as he did so.

'It's OK, dude.' Larry tried to soothe him. 'It's only a film. It's not real life.'

But Boris wouldn't stop.

'Maybe he really doesn't like vampires,' said Harry, turning up the volume to drown out the noise Boris was making. 'Be quiet, Boris, or you'll have to sleep in the kitchen.'

With a final frustrated bark, Boris slumped down beside the door.

'Was that a car outside?' asked Larry.

'No, don't be daft. That's the alien,' replied Harry, pointing at the screen. 'What's the matter? Scared?'

'Shut up!'

'No, you shut up!'

It was long after midnight when the film finally ended. As the boys let Boris out into the hall, he ran to the door and barked again.

'Stop it, Boris,' mumbled Larry, as they staggered upstairs. ''Stime for bed. Come on, boy.'

But Boris wouldn't come. All night long he lay by the front door, whimpering, waiting for someone to notice that all was not well.

Granny Pam was the only one up early enough the next morning to watch *BBC Breakfast*. She let Boris out for his morning pee, but when he came back he was whimpering.

'What's the matter with you, little one?' she asked.

Granny Pam had never had her own dog because her acting had taken her on the road too often, but she had a soft spot for Boris. He always seemed so . . . human. He looked at her now with his head on one side and gave a low whine. Then he looked at the front door and back at her.

'I know, Boris. It's not fair that they've left us all on our own here, is it? Do you miss your Charlie? Is that what it is? Well, let's cuddle up together and watch her on the telly. That's the best I can offer,

I'm afraid. Here's a biscuit as well. Good boy.'

She leaned down and offered him a biscuit, but he refused to take it. He whined again.

'Suit yourself,' she said, shaking her head, then she shouted up the stairs: 'BOYS! Time to get up. They'll be on soon.'

Granny Pam made a cup of tea before settling down in front of the television. It showed a quick shot of Caroline, Bill, Joe and Charlie backstage. Caroline looked slightly alarmed, while Bill was clearly uncomfortable in tight trousers and a brand-new checked shirt. Charlie smiled nervously and waved at the camera. Her hair was styled slightly differently and she looked as if her cheeks had been polished with a cloth. Joe was wearing blue jeans and a white shirt and looked very fresh-faced.

Larry appeared, yawning.

'Is Dad wearing mascara?' he said, as he sat down heavily beside her.

'They've all been made up,' replied Granny Pam. 'For the cameras, darling.'

Soon Charlie, Joe, Caroline and Bill were sitting

awkwardly on a red sofa opposite the presenters, who asked questions about the Derby and showed footage of the race.

'We've also got this angle, which I don't think you've seen before,' said Mike Morgan, as the screens switched to a view from the camera in the blimp floating above the racecourse. It showed Charlie galloping across the middle of the racecourse before she slipped through a gap in the rails and on to the course itself.

'What happened next?' asked Hannah Hooper, the other presenter.

'I realized I was standing too close to the winning post,' Charlie explained. 'If Noble Warrior had seen Percy there, he might have started to slow down before he crossed the line, but I guessed that if I went a bit further down the track, he would keep galloping. I always knew he was fast enough to win the Derby: it was just a case of making him want to do it.'

Charlie looked across at Joe and he picked up her cue.

'It was as if he'd suddenly sprouted wings,' he said, as the screens showed a shot of him raising his whip to the sky. 'I've never felt anything like it and doubt I will again. It really was the best day of my life.'

Mike then asked Charlie what the Queen had said to her in the winner's enclosure and they showed footage of Percy nearly biting her and Bill putting his arm in the way to stop him.

'That pony looks a bit vicious,' laughed Mike. 'You wouldn't want to mess with him.'

'He's very protective of Noble Warrior,' explained Charlie. 'He doesn't like to let anyone get too close to him, not even the Queen.'

The TV now showed footage of the farm and all the people at the Open Day. There were shots of Harry and Larry flapping their arms at the chickens as they tried desperately to make them dance, and a brief glimpse of Granny Pam doing a speech from *Macbeth* in front of a small knot of confused-looking visitors.

'They didn't appreciate the intricacy of the piece,'

Granny Pam muttered to Larry. 'When I gave my Lady Macbeth in Chichester, the director cried with admiration.'

'Is that all they're showing?' asked Harry, who had wandered in halfway through. 'After all the trouble I took organizing the day? Barely a minute's worth of footage.'

'Well, it looks like it was an extraordinary day,' said Hannah, smiling kindly. 'You really have captured the hearts of the nation.'

'But here's the question everyone wants to know the answer to . . .' Mike bent forward and lowered his voice. 'What's Noble Warrior worth now he's won the Derby?'

'Well, we don't want to sell him,' said Charlie calmly, 'so it doesn't really matter what he's worth. There are plenty more races he could run in, like the King George at Ascot, or the Arc in Paris, or even the Breeders' Cup in America, but we really haven't decided yet. He's having a rest and enjoying himself at home and that's the only plan at the moment – keep him fit and healthy and happy.'

'And that's all we've got time for,' said Hannah before Charlie could take another breath. 'Next, we'll be finding out what keeps Lulu looking so young and why it makes you want to shout.'

'And we'll be hearing from President Trump,' continued Mike, 'about why it's best to let the Russians build the wall between the US and Mexico.'

'Well, that wasn't very long,' said Granny Pam disappointedly.

'Tell us about it,' Harry replied. 'They hardly had any of me and Larry, and I can't be the only one who thinks *that* was a mistake.'

Larry yawned again. 'I'm going back to bed. See you later.'

'Me too,' said Harry, as he followed his brother up the stairs.

Granny Pam wandered back into the kitchen to make another cup of tea. The morning papers dropped through the front door and Boris didn't try to pick one up. He just lay there, whining.

Chapter 5

Charlie couldn't get out of the studio fast enough. She grabbed a face wipe from the make-up room and wiped off the brown foundation and powder that had been applied to her face.

'Would you like me to get you a water or some juice?' asked the helpful runner who had been assigned to look after them.

'No thanks,' replied Charlie. 'We really ought to be getting home.'

She didn't like Salford with its cold grey concrete and its tall buildings that had names like Quay House and Dock House. She had barely slept a wink in the hotel because the doors on her floor kept slamming and all night she'd had an uneasy feeling in her stomach.

Charlie didn't know why it was but she felt very odd. Maybe it was because she didn't know how to start another conversation with Joe about the job offer in Ireland.

'We could go into Manchester while we're here,' Caroline suggested. 'There's a People's History Museum I'd love to see.'

'I'd rather not,' Charlie said quietly but firmly as she wiped the last of her make-up off. 'Dad will want to get back for the cows. He hates missing a morning milking and I don't think the boys can manage on their own. It's not that I don't trust them . . .'

'It's just that you don't trust them,' laughed Caroline, completing her daughter's sentence.

Charlie couldn't deny it.

'It's just best if Joe and I take the horses out. I can't imagine what Harry and Larry would think is suitable exercise. I'll probably find them teaching Percy the cha-cha-cha.'

'Fair enough,' replied Caroline. 'You're the trainer and I'm sure we'll be back here another time.'

'Not if I've got anything to do with it,' Charlie murmured, as she headed for the lifts. She didn't like being away from the farm and she hadn't enjoyed the interview. It was as if they didn't listen to anything she said but just moved from one planned question to the next. The only good bit was being able to watch Joe's celebrations again. She'd liked that, but, whenever she'd caught sight of herself on one of the screens, she'd shuddered. She looked weird, not at all like herself. She wondered how Granny Pam could have been such a natural performer while Charlie and her mother didn't like being in front of an audience at all.

As they were driven back down the M6, Joe and Charlie steered clear of the subject of Seamus

O'Reilly's letter by discussing Noble Warrior's summer and autumn options. The question with most Derby winners was whether to stick to a mile and a half, move up to a mile and three-quarters or drop back to a mile and a quarter. But with Noble Warrior, the real question was the shape of the racecourse.

For Percy to be able to accompany Noddy to the start and still get to the finish line before him, the track had to be circular or horseshoe-shaped, with a route to cut across the middle. Noble Warrior might be able to gallop with the other racehorses once he'd started a race, but, for him to want to finish in front of them, Charlie knew he still needed to see Percy ahead of him, waiting on the other side of the winning line.

'I went to Ascot once with my dad,' said Joe. 'If we ran in the King George, I reckon you could get to the finishing post before us. You'd just turn Percy round at the start and go backwards round the course. It's only a couple of furlongs from there so it should be fine. York is big and open in the middle, and the finish is almost directly opposite the start so that's fine.'

'Goodwood is out of the question,' Charlie offered. 'I saw it on the TV and it's not a circle. It's really pretty and there's a big field with lots of trees in the middle, but it's no good for us because there isn't a route through them.'

As they continued to debate different race-courses, Charlie almost forgot the nausea that had been building up inside her, but, as they got closer to home, she began to feel a sense of dread overtaking her.

'Do you mind if I open the window?' she asked the driver. 'I'm feeling a bit sick.'

The driver nodded and slowed down.

'No, no, don't slow down,' Charlie said. 'I need to get home as soon as possible. Something's wrong, I just know it.'

As they turned into Folly Farm, they all heard barking. Boris was running down the drive to meet them, as he often did. Usually he would wag his tail and bark with delight, but this morning he looked frantic and angry. He kept running towards the farmyard and running back again. As the chauffeur parked the car, Boris ran towards the barn and back again, barking all the time.

'What's his problem?' asked Joe.

'I don't know,' said Charlie. 'But I don't like it.'

Joe and Charlie followed Boris and, as they turned the corner, they froze. The gate to the barn was hanging open, swaying in the wind.

Boris had run ahead and was already inside the huge open stall that Noble Warrior and Percy shared. Charlie and Joe followed him warily, unsure of what they would find. When they got to the barn, they saw Percy lying on his side, breathing heavily. There were six banana skins on the straw beside him. Charlie kneeled next to him, running her hand along his tummy, which seemed bloated and tight. Boris sniffed at Percy's head and whimpered.

'You poor lad,' Charlie said softly, as Percy groaned. 'What's happened to you?'

It was then that she realized there was something

missing. Percy's best friend would normally be right by his side. He hated to be parted from him, so where was he now? Where was Noble Warrior? Charlie swallowed hard, trying not to be sick. No wonder she had felt so anxious all morning. She looked at Joe and saw her panic reflected in his eyes.

'Joe, you stay here with Percy. I'll go and look.' Charlie sounded calmer than she felt. Her heart was hammering against her chest so hard she thought it might burst out through her ribs.

She ran outside and looked in the field, ran back and searched the area the pigs lived in, even checking in their pigsties. She sprinted past the chickens and scoured the farmyard. The cows had filed into the milking shed, where Bill was already busy milking them in turn, apologizing to each one for having been late.

'He's disappeared, Joe,' Charlie said on her return. 'There's no sign of him anywhere.'

Joe was soothing Percy, cradling his head in his lap. He had a bucket of water next to him and was

dipping his hand into it, trying to encourage Percy to drink from the palm of his hand.

'It's all my fault,' he said mournfully. 'I shouldn't have gone to Salford with you. I should've been here with the horses and the cows. I'm a farmhand, not a jockey, and I shouldn't fool myself.'

'Stop it, Joe. Stop it right this minute!' Charlie shocked herself with the sternness of her own voice. 'You *are* a jockey and you had every right to be talking on TV about winning the Derby. This is not your fault and I'm not going to let you blame yourself or think any differently about your future because of it.'

She looked at Boris, who was whining softly.

'I bet you knew something was up, didn't you?' Charlie asked him. 'Why didn't anyone listen to you? Well, we'd better start making some calls.' Charlie's voice was softer now. She felt guilty for snapping at Joe. 'We'll find a way to sort this out, I promise.'

Charlie marched back to the house.

'Call a vet!' she shouted, as she went inside.

'A vet? What on earth is going on?' Granny Pam looked alarmed.

'Percy's been poisoned and Noble Warrior has disappeared.'

'What?' Granny Pam started to fan herself with a tea towel. 'Oh my Lord, that's awful. I must sit down.'

'We have to call the vet.' Charlie looked around the room and was relieved to see her mother with the phone in her hand.

'I'm on to it,' she said.

'Granny Pam, where are the boys?' asked Charlie. 'They were meant to be in charge.'

'Well, they came down to watch you all on the television. You were MARVELLOUS, by the way. Simply MARVELLOUS. Then they went back to bed. I watched the rest of *BBC Breakfast* and then it was *Homes Under the Hammer* and I'm afraid I got rather sucked in, and then there you were, all of you, back again. I should have checked on the horses, but I've really never been terribly good with animals, not like you, Charlie.'

Caroline had taken the phone next door to talk to the vet. She came back into the room to hear the end of her mother's explanation.

'It's all right, Mum. It really wasn't your fault. The boys should've been helping you, not sleeping the morning away. The vet's coming,' she added. 'She'll only be a few minutes. I told her it was an emergency.'

'I'll go back out and stay with Percy until she gets here,' Charlie said. 'But we need to work out how on earth this happened.'

Charlie crossed the yard back to the stable, kneeled down beside Joe and started rubbing Percy's tummy. She took deep, loud breaths, trying to encourage Percy to copy her.

'You poor old thing,' she said softly, as she massaged him. 'The vet's coming.'

Percy's ear flicked as if he understood.

'He looks like he's been given some sort of tranquillizer to knock him out,' Joe said.

Charlie glanced at the banana skins.

'They must have injected it into the bananas to make it easier to get it into him. Poor boy.'

'Who would've done such a thing?' Joe asked. 'And what have they done with Noddy?'

Charlie had been trying to think as clearly as she could and one theory kept popping into her mind. It was the worst thing she could imagine, and part of her didn't even want to say it out loud, but, if she couldn't say it to Joe, she would never be able to suggest it to anyone else.

'I think . . .' she faltered. 'I don't know why or who or how, but I have a horrible feeling that he might've been kidnapped.'

Joe looked at her, his eyes wide with fear.

'Why do you think that? Couldn't he just have got scared and run off in the dark? We'll probably find him in the woods or by the stream or over the hill with the cows . . .'

His voice trailed off. With any other horse that might be a possibility, but not this one.

They were both thinking the same thing. If Noble Warrior wasn't with Percy then he must have been taken away. He would never, ever choose to leave his best friend.

'It's because he's so valuable,' said Charlie, feeling tears fill her eyes. 'He's the Derby winner. He's worth millions.'

'But only if he's a racehorse,' replied Joe. 'He's not worth anything at all to people who don't know how to get the best out of him. He was only worth a thousand pounds when you bought him, because no one else had been able to make him gallop.'

'Those men,' Charlie said quietly. 'The two men who were at the Open Day yesterday. The whispering one and the one in the baseball cap. They were asking me about Percy's favourite food and I told them he loved bananas. Boris really didn't like the two of them, and I just thought he was being rude, but maybe he was trying to warn me.'

'I remember them,' said Charlie's dad, who had appeared at the entrance to the stall. 'I brought them here and showed them where the horses lived. Showed them round the whole farm, how the gate opened and everything. They were particularly interested in the cattle truck.'

'The cattle truck . . .' said Charlie slowly.

'Yes, they wanted to know if it started all right and whether it had a noisy engine. I thought it was a bit odd, but they said they were thinking of buying it from me second hand.'

'Where is the cattle truck?' Charlie asked. 'I didn't see it when we got back. Have you moved it, Dad?'

'No, I left it right in the middle of the yard yesterday. Right there –' Bill pointed at a space in the yard. A space in which there was no cattle truck. 'Oh, no . . .'

Charlie sat in silence for the next ten minutes. She tried to calm herself by concentrating on her breathing and rubbing Percy's tummy in smooth, rhythmical strokes. *Think logically*, she said to herself. Finally, she spoke out loud.

'We need to call the BBC. That footage they shot at the Open Day yesterday: those two men might be in it somewhere. We need to find a clear image so we know who we're looking for. Also,' continued Charlie, 'we should call Mr and Mrs Williams. They know everyone in the racing world and, if someone tries to sell Noddy on, they'll hear about it. Plus, I need to tell Polly so that she doesn't find out from someone else.'

At that moment, the vet arrived to examine Percy. She took his heart rate and his temperature, inserting the thermometer into his bottom. Percy flattened his ears back and looked grumpy.

'That's a good sign,' said Charlie. 'He's more like his old self.'

'He seems stable. He's clearly got a very strong constitution,' said the vet. 'But we'll have to lavage his stomach.'

Charlie frowned. She didn't know what that meant.

'Wash it through with water,' explained the vet. 'To get as much of the tranquillizer out of his system as we can. I'll give him a solution of magnesium sulphate, which will act as a laxative. That'll help matters along. I can administer it through a tube directly into his stomach, but it's better if he drinks it himself.'

Charlie and Joe stayed with Percy while the vet treated him. Charlie held the bucket and encouraged him to drink, while the vet examined the banana skins.

'What do you think they used to knock him out?' asked Joe.

'Looks to me like it could be Domosedan,' said the vet, holding up the evidence. 'You can see traces of the blue gel here on the skin. Clever. It's fast-acting, but it's meant to be placed under the tongue, not swallowed. No wonder Percy's still feeling groggy. It looks as if he's had a massive dose of it.'

Percy took a drink of water and then another. His tummy tensed and his eyes widened. Then he lifted his tail and let out the biggest trumpet they had ever heard, followed by a stream of very runny poo.

'That's it, Percy,' said Charlie, smiling for the first time in hours. 'You get rid of all that nasty stuff. Go on, let it out.'

Percy seemed more relaxed and comfortable after his bottom explosion. He struggled to his feet and stood with his head hanging low. For once, he didn't frisk Charlie's pockets for titbits. He didn't seem in the mood to eat.

'I think you can leave him for a while,' said Joe, tapping Charlie's arm. 'He probably just wants some peace and quiet. I don't think he'll be after any more bananas in a hurry. I wonder if they gave Noddy some of that gel as well, to get him into the cattle truck.'

'Well, if they did,' said Charlie, 'it will have worn off by now and he'll be kicking up an almighty storm.'

Leaving Joe in the barn, Charlie headed back to the kitchen and picked up the phone. She tapped in Polly's home number and waited as it rang eight times. It went to answerphone so Charlie hung up.

'That's odd,' she said to herself. 'There's always someone at the house in the mornings.'

She tried the office number instead.

'Good morning, Cherrydown Stables, this is Sheila speaking.' The voice was brisk and efficient.

'Hello, Sheila, it's Polly's friend Charlie here. Is Mr Williams there? I need to talk to him about something that's happened to Noble Warrior.'

There was a pause and Charlie could hear Sheila swallow, as if she wanted to say something but couldn't.

'Charlie, how nice to hear from you. I'm afraid Mr Williams isn't, um, actually here at the moment. He's, ah, he's with Polly and Mrs Williams.' Sheila stopped again and Charlie could hear her blowing her nose. 'I'll tell them that you called,' she said, before hanging up.

'That was strange,' Charlie said to her mother.

'Sheila – their racing secretary – sounded upset about something. She said Mr and Mrs Williams aren't there. They've gone somewhere with Polly.'

'Well, don't worry about it now,' said Caroline. 'You can try them again later. I've called the police and they promised they'd be here in the next half-hour. Let's focus on what we can tell them that might help narrow down where Noddy's been taken.'

Charlie nodded. She had to deal with one thing at a time and, now that Percy was on the mend, the next thing was to try to work out who had taken Noble Warrior and where they might be heading.

'We need that footage from the Open Day,' she said purposefully. 'Can you call the BBC, Mum? I need to talk to Harry and Larry. Where are they anyway?'

'They must still be in bed,' said Caroline, as she marched out of the kitchen. 'Harry! Larry! Get up, *right now*!' She shouted up the stairs.

Charlie could feel a seething anger growing inside her. Her brothers were meant to have been in charge of the farm, not lazing in bed. She tapped her fingers on the kitchen table, drumming faster and faster as her rage built up. There was a crashing and banging from the boys' rooms and then uneven footsteps on the stairs. Harry came in first, rubbing his eyes, followed by Larry, who looked wary. Charlie glared at them and pointed at the chairs on the other side of the table.

'What's this, an interrogation?' said Harry.

Larry put his hand out to his older brother to try to quieten him down.

'What is it, Charlie?' he asked.

Boris stuck like a limpet to Charlie's left leg and stared at the boys, then up at Charlie. Finally, she spoke.

'I would like to know, if you don't mind, what exactly you two were up to last night when thieves broke into our farm, stole the cattle truck and kidnapped Noble Warrior?'

Harry's cocky air vanished. His mouth started opening and closing of its own accord. Only one word came out.

'What?'

'You heard me,' replied Charlie coldly. 'What were you two doing while our precious racehorse was being stolen?'

'That's why Boris was barking,' Larry said. 'And I told you I heard something. You said it was just the film.'

'I did not say that, you liar,' Harry retorted.

'Did so!'

'Did not –'

'SHUT UP!' shouted Charlie. 'Shut up, the pair of you! You were meant to be in charge! You were meant to check the horses last thing at night and feed them this morning and you didn't. You obviously just watched TV until it was so late that you collapsed into bed. You ignored Boris, who was clearly trying to tell you something was wrong, and I'm telling you this now – I am holding *you* responsible and, if we don't find Noddy, it will all be *your fault*!'

Turning on her heel, Charlie ran out of the kitchen, tears pouring down her face.

Outside in the fresh air, she took a deep breath. Shouting at her brothers might have made her feel better for a moment, but it wouldn't help get Noddy back or make Percy better. It was all hopeless. Just hopeless. Boris jumped up at her leg and she picked him up to let him comfort her. He licked away the tears on her cheeks.

In the barn, Percy was warm with sweat and his head was still hanging low, but he looked up as Charlie came in and flicked his ears forward. Joe was holding a bucket of water and encouraging him to drink.

'He's on the mend,' Joe said. 'And at least he's steadier on his feet now. The vet's given him some electrolytes to help him recover and we've got to make him drink a bit more. I think he's in shock.'

'I don't blame him,' said Charlie, as she stroked Percy's neck. 'I think we all are.'

'Are you OK?' asked Joe.

'Not really,' replied Charlie. 'I've just yelled at Harry and Larry. If they'd been paying more attention to the animals and not watching some silly film, they might have heard the thieves. They could've called the police or something. They just don't care about anyone except themselves.'

'Oh, I don't know,' replied Joe. 'They might not show it, but I think they care about Noddy too. I expect they've been stung into action and will be searching high and low for clues.'

Percy looked around the barn and, for the first time, seemed to realize he was on his own. He let out a low, soft whinny.

'He's not here, my love,' Charlie explained. 'But we'll find him.'

Percy gave another whinny and dropped his head.

Charlie felt like crying again. She had never seen Percy look so lost. He always seemed the confident one, the one who didn't really need a friend but put up with Noble Warrior's devotion because it meant he got well fed. Now she realized that their love was mutual. It made her even more determined to act quickly and stop the kidnappers before they got too far away.

'Those two blokes asked me some funny questions as well,' said Joe. 'The whispering one wanted to know whether Noddy had ever pulled a trap.'

'Pulled a trap?' Charlie looked confused. 'What did he mean?'

'You know those racing carriages? Small and light, a bit like a Roman chariot. That's what I think he meant anyway. Strange thing to ask.'

'They asked me that too,' Charlie suddenly remembered. 'They called it a cart, but I guess they mean the same thing.'

Suddenly Charlie felt overwhelmed. She had tried so hard not to let emotion overtake her. All the books she had read about what makes Olympians special had emphasized the need to let the head rule the heart, not to get carried away by the situation or the setting or the opposition or the history, just to stay in the moment and play the game. This wasn't a game she had ever wanted to play, but the same rules applied. It was just so difficult to think clearly when she was so scared.

Joe put his arm round her shoulder as they walked back towards the farmhouse, Boris trotting alongside them.

'The police should be here soon,' he said. 'The sooner we can get on the trail of the cattle truck, the better.'

In the kitchen, Harry and Larry were sitting at the table, looking at a large envelope.

'Don't touch it!' exclaimed Larry. 'There might be fingerprints.'

'I won't, you idiot,' snapped Harry. 'I've seen just as many detective films as you have.'

'Don't start fighting again, boys,' said Caroline. 'Let Charlie decide what to do.'

'We went to look for tyre tracks and found it at the end of the drive,' explained Larry. 'It was leaning up against the gatepost. The thieves must have left it before they drove off.'

The envelope was addressed to THE OWNER OF NOBLE WARRIOR.

Charlie put on a pair of washing-up gloves to open it carefully. Inside was a single piece of paper

covered in cut-out letters from newspapers. Charlie
read it aloud:

A million
pounds or
Your horse
is dog meAT

Chapter 6

'It's just like what happened to Shergar,' said Bill Bass, shaking his head.

Charlie looked at him with furrowed brows. She knew the name.

'Remember when we were going through the videos of past Derbies, Joe?' asked Bill. 'He's the one that was so far clear that the jockey on the second horse thought *he'd* won.'

Joe nodded.

'So what happened to him?' Charlie asked.

'He was an amazing horse. He was owned by the Aga Khan, one of the most powerful men in the world, and ridden by one of the most talented jockeys you'll ever see – Walter Swinburn. He was only nineteen when he rode him in the 1981 Derby and he was brilliant. They called him 'the Choirboy' because he looked so angelic.

'Anyway, Shergar hit the front miles from home. He came up the straight almost on his own and the crowd clapped all through the last furlong. It was amazing. He won the Irish Derby in a hack canter too, barely looking as if he was trying, and won the King George at Ascot as well. Then he ran in the St Leger at Doncaster, but he got beaten.'

The boys were all ears. They had been trying to talk Charlie into running Noble Warrior in the King George and perhaps the St Leger as well.

'He was retired to stud, valued at ten million pounds,' Bill continued. 'So the Aga Khan syndicated him – like you would with a company – selling thirty-four shares in him. His vet even bought one of the shares.'

'Must've been a rich vet!' said Larry.

'Or maybe he twigged it was a good investment,' said Charlie. 'After all, he'd know how fit Shergar was and how big his heart was and whether he could pass that on to his offspring. If he was right, he would stand to make tens of millions.'

'Sadly,' said Bill, 'he never got the chance to find out. Neither did the other shareholders.'

'Why? What happened?' Harry was desperate to know how the story ended.

'Shergar was kidnapped. A gang of men, dressed as Irish police officers with balaclavas on, came to the stud. They took the stud groom at gunpoint and forced him to load Shergar into a horsebox. Then they drove the groom around for a few hours before they pushed him out on to a back road somewhere. He never knew where they'd taken the horse.

'The kidnappers asked the Aga Khan for two million pounds as a ransom. They didn't realize that he didn't own the horse any more, or not all of him anyway. Or that the Aga Khan would never agree to pay a ransom because, if he did, every racehorse in Ireland and England would become a target for kidnappers.'

Charlie looked down at the note and back at her father.

'Did they get Shergar back?'

Bill glanced at his wife and puffed out his cheeks.

'No, love, they didn't. The police never found him and they never caught the kidnappers. It's one of the great unsolved mysteries.'

The boys were silent. Charlie looked pale. Eventually, she spoke very deliberately.

'Well, our story is not going to end like that. We're going to find Noble Warrior. We're going to get him back. If that means we have to raise the money to pay them, we'll do it.'

'I'm so sorry. I know this is all our fault,' Harry said.

'Yeah,' added Larry sheepishly. 'We should have listened to Boris.'

Charlie stared at her brothers, but said nothing. She was still furious with them and wasn't prepared to let them off the hook that easily.

'We need to find the cattle truck,' Harry said. 'Dad, did they do that in Ireland when Shergar was taken? Did they try to track the horsebox?'

'They did,' said Bill, 'but the kidnappers had been very clever. They'd chosen a day when the big sales were on and hundreds of horseboxes were on the roads, so the police could never get an accurate sighting.'

'Hmm . . .' Charlie was thinking. 'What time did Boris start barking last night?'

Harry and Larry shuffled in their chairs and looked down at the table.

'Um, I don't know,' muttered Harry. 'About midnight, I think.' He shifted again in his chair.

'Midnight!' exclaimed Caroline. 'What on earth were you two still doing up at midnight?'

'They told me they were following me straight up to bed, darling. I had no reason to disbelieve them and I'm afraid I didn't hear a thing.' Granny Pam pointed to her hearing aid. 'Took it out to help me sleep. I'm SO sorry.'

'Granny Pam, you don't have anything to be sorry

about. Nobody is blaming you,' Charlie said pointedly.

'So, it was pitch-dark,' said Bill. 'Well, that means they won't have got very far in the cattle truck.'

'Why not?' asked Charlie.

'The headlights don't work. I was going to get them mended, but then I figured that if we were selling the truck the new owners could do that for themselves.'

'How far do you think they could have got?' asked Caroline.

'To the end of the drive and possibly along the lane, but they couldn't have driven on the main road, not without headlights. It would be too dangerous. I reckon they might have got to the lay-by up the road, but then they'd have to wait there for sunrise. Oh, and another thing,' continued Bill. 'The truck only had about a quarter of a tank of diesel left, so they won't get much further than sixty miles or so before they'll need to stop at a garage.'

'Right,' said Charlie. 'Harry, you get working on

the iPad. I knew it would come in handy for something other than vlogging. Have a look at Google Maps and find all the garages within sixty miles of here.'

'Will do,' said Harry. 'It should be easy enough to find a phone number for each one too. Larry, you'll help me do that, won't you?'

Larry nodded and Charlie marvelled at her brothers' ability to transform from complete idiots into useful human beings (and often back again) in an instant.

'Don't you think we should let the police do all of this?' asked Caroline. 'They're on their way here to talk to us.'

Granny Pam was washing up mugs in the sink. She had been listening carefully.

'Oh, I wouldn't do that, dear,' she said. 'As I recall from the Shergar kidnapping, that was the mistake they made. They left it all to the police, and some detective called "Spud" made a COMPLETE mess of it all. I reckon we need to handle as much as we can ourselves. Sometimes the only way to get the job done is to do it yourself.'

She put a mug on to the draining board with a thud.

'Good point, Granny Pam. You're a star,' said Charlie.

'I was once, my dear. Not any more, but I was once. I played Miss Marple on tour. I might have to channel some of her deduction skills to solve this one.'

Boris started barking and when Charlie looked out of the window there was a police car negotiating its way down the drive.

'Good lad, Boris. You hear everything, don't you?' She patted his head and then looked sideways at her brothers, who were poring over the iPad and writing down phone numbers. 'Not like some people.'

Harry and Larry were shamefaced. They picked up the iPad and sloped out of the room.

'I know you're angry, sweetheart,' said Caroline. 'And I know it can make you feel better to blame someone, but it's not always helpful. We need to find the people who did this and, whatever Harry and Larry's faults, they did not commit the crime. You need to stay calm and solve the problem, not get angry and shut them out when they could still be helpful. It's not easy, but you have to try.'

There was a thunderous knock at the door, followed by a loud voice saying, 'POLICE! Open up.'

Charlie jumped up to let in the two police officers. Both of them were in uniform; one had a hat under his arm, the other kept hers on her head. He was very tall, well over six foot, and she was smaller, maybe five foot five. They showed their badges and the woman said: 'My name is Chief Inspector Catherine Bronks and this is Sergeant Christopher Bronks.'

The Chief Inspector's cold tone of voice made Charlie nervous, as if she herself was under suspicion.

'We've been called to investigate the disappearance of . . .' Sergeant Bronks hesitated as he looked at his notepad. 'A horse and a truck.'

'Yes, that's right.' Charlie showed the two officers into the kitchen, looking from one to the other. They bore a striking resemblance.

'A bit confusing, I realize,' said the Chief Inspector. 'Us both being called Bronks. He's my brother, you see. Joined the force a few years after I did. Couldn't bear being away from your big sister, could you?'

Chief Inspector Bronks cuffed Sergeant Bronks round the ear, like a lion cub playing with a littermate. Sergeant Bronks didn't look amused.

'That's right, Chief. Couldn't keep away;' he said, adding under his breath, 'believe me, I've tried.'

'Would you like a cup of tea, officers?' asked Mrs Bass anxiously. 'A flapjack?'

She held out a plate of blackened oat bricks.

'No thank you,' said the Chief Inspector. 'Just a cup of tea would be lovely, Mrs Bass.'

The sergeant also waved away the flapjacks but accepted tea, with four teaspoons of sugar.

'So,' said the Chief Inspector, slapping a large notepad on to the table and pulling out a chair, 'let's start at the beginning. What kind of a horse is it?'

She sat down with a thud and slurped noisily at her tea while Sergeant Bronks stayed standing.

Charlie explained that Noble Warrior was a thoroughbred and described his colour and his markings.

'Most distinctive, though, is his behaviour. He's a very nervous horse and he hates being anywhere

without his best friend Percy, who's a pony. Noble Warrior will be extremely agitated on his own.'

The police officers looked at one another.

'We had reports of an accident this morning caused by a truck, possibly carrying an animal of some sort' said Sergeant Bronks. 'A young girl was badly injured.'

Charlie looked surprised.

'Where was this?'

'We are not at liberty to tell you that, miss,' replied Chief Inspector Bronks firmly. 'Now if we could return to your case. You say the cattle truck was stolen in the early hours of this morning. Could you describe it for us, please.'

'It's an Iveco Fiat livestock truck – 1976. Blue and grey. The back tail light is smashed and the headlights don't work. Registration YFC 749R.'

As Sergeant Bronks painstakingly noted the details Charlie was giving, Charlie began to feel exasperated. She knew that, for every minute spent talking, Noddy and the cattle truck were another mile further away.

'My brothers are currently contacting the nearby garages to see if it's come in to refuel. It only had a quarter of a tank of diesel so it'll need to fill up soon.'

The Chief Inspector looked impressed.

'There's also this.' Charlie pointed at the ransom note. 'We found it at the bottom of the drive.'

The Chief Inspector and her brother leaned over the note to examine it more closely.

'Old-fashioned newsprint, eh? Not exactly cutting-edge technology,' said Sergeant Bronks. 'Suggests to me they aren't professional kidnappers.'

'We can't afford to pay a million-pound ransom,' said Charlie. 'But if we offer them some of it they might agree, mightn't they?'

'I wouldn't advise that, miss,' said the Chief Inspector coolly. 'In our experience, the offer to pay a ransom does not always result in the satisfactory return of the stolen person or item. Or, in this case, animal. Paying the ransom is not the approach we would recommend, even if you could afford the whole amount.

It sends a bad signal, I'm afraid.'

'But surely, if we give them what *they* want, they'll give us back what *we* want,' replied Charlie desperately. Boris nudged her leg and she leaned down to stroke his head. He always knew when she needed his support.

'Not necessarily,' said Sergeant Bronks. 'More often than not, paying a ransom only encourages the kidnappers to come back for more. Leave it with us, miss. We've done this sort of thing before.'

'Do you mind if I ask HOW MANY times you've done this sort of thing before?' Granny Pam had been eyeing the two police officers with suspicion. 'And with what success rate?'

'No, ma'am, you may not ask that.' The Chief Inspector cut her off, standing abruptly. 'We need to get going. In most solved kidnapping cases, the victim is found within the first forty-eight hours. After that, the chances of success fall dramatically.'

She shut her notepad and marched to the front door, followed by her brother, leaving the ransom note on the table.

'Just one very serious word of advice,' she said, as she walked out. 'Leave this to us and do *not* pay that ransom.'

Chapter 7

As the police car disappeared down the drive, Charlie bunched her fists in frustration. Sitting at home doing nothing did not come naturally to her.

She sat at the kitchen table and looked out of the window. She could see Elvis and Doris snuffling for food in their pigpen. Beyond them, the cows were in their big field, munching grass, and, in the barn, she knew that Percy would soon be back to his greedy ways.

She wondered what Noble Warrior was doing now, whether the whispering man and the weird, smiling man in the baseball cap were feeding him properly, giving him water and keeping him calm. She knew he would be very unhappy and upset because Percy wasn't with him, and confused because he wouldn't know the men who had taken him.

'How are you doing, chicken?' Bill Bass sat down next to his daughter. 'Don't you worry. We will sort this out, I promise you.'

'What if it ends up like Shergar?' asked Charlie, her voice cracking with fear and sadness. 'What if we never find him or the kidnappers?'

A tear slid down her cheek.

Before her father could answer, Charlie's mum came into the kitchen, looking shocked.

'Mum, what's wrong?' asked Charlie.

'Jasmine Williams just called,' Caroline said falteringly. 'That accident the police mentioned – it happened just outside Cherrydown. Polly's pony was spooked by a truck driving too fast. Munchkin reared up and flipped backwards, trapping Polly underneath her.'

'What happened?' Charlie gasped. 'Is Polly hurt? Mum, you have to tell me.'

Caroline took Charlie's hand.

'Yes, darling, she is. She's in the hospital. She was knocked unconscious and it looks as if her injuries could be very serious indeed.'

'Oh, no, poor Polly!'

'Would you like to go and see her?' asked Bill. 'We could go to the hospital. At least then you'll know how she is.'

Charlie's throat had tightened up so much she couldn't speak, but she nodded. Polly had been her best friend since their first day at primary school. They had bonded over their love of horses and Polly was the only one who hadn't teased Charlie about living on a farm and smelling of cows. She couldn't bear the thought of her being injured. And if this was all connected with Noble Warrior's kidnap then it was even worse.

Charlie didn't trust the police to find the cattle

truck, but she and her family couldn't start chasing after it on their own. They had no idea where it had gone. The only thing she could do right now was try to offer Polly some support. She would have to trust her brothers to find out more information while she went to the hospital.

She looked round the door of the library to see the boys sitting cross-legged on the floor among piles of her mother's books. They had the iPad between them and were writing down the phone number of every garage in the area.

'Broadband's gone again,' groaned Larry. 'It's useless. This is going to take ages. If only we knew which direction they're going.'

Charlie walked quickly back to the kitchen and stared again at the ransom note. The typeface of the letters was different from the newspapers she knew.

'Harry!' she shouted. 'Have you still got all those papers from around the country that you collected the day after the Derby?'

'Yup,' came the reply. 'Do you want me to get them?'

'Yes,' called Charlie. 'I'm wondering if we can match the typeface. It might give us a clue.'

They laid the papers out on the table and held them next to the ransom demand, one by one.

'That's a match!' cried Larry, clutching the *Tavistock Times Gazette*.

'So is this one!' Harry waved the *Yorkshire Post*.

'This one too.' Granny Pam moved the *Lancashire Telegraph* into the centre of the table.

'And this one.' Larry was looking at the *Essex Chronicle*.

'Well, that doesn't narrow it down much,' said Charlie, staring at the newspapers and at the ransom note. 'They could be heading north or east or west.'

She sighed long and hard. They didn't even know where to start looking. It was all she could do not to fall into complete despair.

'I'll keep thinking,' Charlie said. 'But before I do anything else, I need to see Polly, if they'll let me.'

'Of course you do, my love,' said Granny Pam. 'You send her our love and tell her we're on the case. We'll find the people who did this to her and, if I have my way, they won't know what's HIT them.'

Granny Pam made a swinging action as if she was wielding a sword.

'I did a bit of stage fighting once when I was with the Royal Shakespeare Company. Never lost it. Swoosh, swoosh and take THAT!'

Granny Pam lunged forward with her imaginary sword and Charlie jumped backwards.

'Well, they'd better watch out then,' Charlie said with a small smile, as she headed to the safer territory of her dad's car.

When they arrived at the hospital, Charlie approached the reception desk at Accident and Emergency.

'Please could you tell me where I can find Polly Williams? She was brought in this morning after a fall from her pony.'

The receptionist tapped at a keyboard and looked at her computer.

'Miss Polly Williams? She's in the ICU. Are you family?'

'Not exactly,' said Charlie. 'She's my best friend. What's the ICU?'

'Intensive Care Unit,' replied the receptionist. 'It's through those doors behind me, but you won't be allowed to see her. Family only. Next, please.'

Intensive Care. It must be bad. Charlie swallowed hard.

'Come on, Charlie,' said her dad. 'We'll come back tomorrow.'

Just at that moment, a person Charlie recognized came through the doors. It was Jasmine Williams. Her face was blotchy and her eyes looked red.

'Charlie!' she exclaimed, hugging her tightly. 'What are you doing here?'

'Mum told me about Polly's accident. I had to come and see her.'

'That's so kind of you, Charlie,' said Mrs Williams. 'It's meant to be family only, but you're like a sister to her, so you can come in for a minute if your dad says it's OK.'

'Can I, Dad?' asked Charlie.

Her dad nodded. 'Just for a minute, mind. And you do just what Mrs Williams tells you. I'll wait here.'

Mrs Williams led the way into the ICU. There seemed to be different rooms and cubicles with curtains separating them. Charlie glanced into the first one to see an old man attached to a machine. He was asleep and breathing heavily, making a sound like sandpaper being dragged over a piece of wood. A woman who must have been his wife was sitting in a chair next to him. Charlie quickened her step to keep up with Mrs Williams, who led her behind the second set of curtains.

When she walked into the cubicle, Charlie gasped. Polly was lying on her back in a big hospital bed. Her head was in a brace, holding it still, and there were straps across her body. A tube ran from her arm into a bag hanging from a metal rail above her head. Beside the bed, a machine beeped every couple of seconds and showed a green graph with peaks and troughs like a mountain range.

Alex Williams was sitting next to his daughter, holding her hand. His face was drawn and pale. Mrs Williams joined him and whispered softly in his ear. Charlie stopped a metre from the bed. She didn't know what to say or do. She didn't want to touch Polly in case she hurt her and yet she wanted to let her know she was here. The beeping continued and Charlie felt as if it was the only sign that time was passing. Like everything else in the world had stopped, apart from the *beep, beep, beep* of the machine.

Charlie had never seen anyone unconscious before, so she tried to imagine that Polly was just asleep. Yes, just taking a nap while her body repaired itself. Charlie smiled at the comforting thought and moved towards the bed. She put her hand on Polly's arm, just above the bandages that had tubes coming out of them. She felt the warmth of Polly's body and tried to transmit positive energy from her hand.

'Hello, Polly. You look . . . lovely. Considering.' Charlie stopped and let out a nervous laugh.

Whatever she said just sounded so stupid. 'Sorry. Not the right thing to say.'

Suddenly Polly's eyelids flickered, then opened.

'Hi, Charlie,' she said weakly. 'Hi, Mum and Dad.'

Mr and Mrs Williams smiled with relief and gripped each other.

'How are you doing, darling?' Mr Williams asked.

'I've felt better,' said Polly. Her eyes closed again and she smiled.

Mr Williams let out an enormous breath.

'Well, thank goodness you're awake,' he said, patting her hand. 'I'll get the nurse.'

Charlie looked at Mr Williams's kind face as he stood up. He seemed to have aged since she last saw him and his eyes were bloodshot. He gestured to his seat, and Charlie slid into it and took Polly's hand.

'You'll be OK, Polly. I know you will. You're the toughest and bravest person I've ever met. You've always stuck up for me and I promise I will do whatever I can to help you get better.'

'Is Munchkin all right?' Polly mumbled.

'Yes, darling, she's fine,' said Jasmine. 'She has a few cuts and bruises, that's all. Trust you to be more worried about your pony than yourself.'

'Can you remember what happened?' asked Charlie gently.

Polly closed her eyes.

'There was a truck. It was going really fast and there was this noise from the back. I think that's what spooked Munchkin so much. It was awful.'

'It's OK. Take your time,' said Charlie, squeezing Polly's hand. 'You don't have to say it all at once.'

'The doctor's on her way,' said Mr Williams, as he came back into the cubicle. 'Has she said anything else?'

'She's just trying to remember about the accident,' Mrs Williams explained.

'Surely she doesn't need to do that now? It'll only upset her.'

'I think I might know what happened,' said Charlie gently.

'What do you mean?' asked Mr Williams.

'Noble Warrior has been kidnapped,' Charlie explained. 'The thieves came in the middle of the night and took him in the cattle truck. But they couldn't have driven very far at night because the headlights don't work. So, once the sun came up, they would have been speeding, trying to get away. And Noddy would have been kicking up a fuss in the back.'

Charlie spoke calmly and she did suddenly feel composed. What had happened to Polly had somehow focused her mind and she knew she must not panic or reveal how terrified she felt for Noble

Warrior. She had to be strong for Polly.

'The truck that sped past you, did it look like ours?' Charlie asked slowly.

Polly furrowed her brow, trying to remember.

'I'm not sure. I think it was grey and blue though. Munchkin started rearing and I couldn't see properly. I was trying to hang on. I heard the banging noise from the back of the truck and I knew it was going too fast, but that's all.'

Polly closed her eyes. She looked exhausted.

'All right, darling, that's enough. You just settle down.' Mrs Williams took Polly's hand again.

'I think you'd better go, Charlie,' said Mr Williams. 'Polly needs to rest and it sounds like you've got other things to worry about. I'll walk you out.'

Charlie leaned forward again and whispered in Polly's ear. 'You stay strong,' she said. 'I'll be back to see you very soon and I promise I'll find who did this to you. Best friends forever.'

She touched Polly's hand again and left the cubicle. Mr Williams came with her.

'Thanks so much for coming, Charlie. I know it will have meant the world to Polly. She's so fond of you. She's always talking about how much she admires what you've done with Noble Warrior.' He gulped and Charlie saw his shoulders sink. His clothes seemed to be hanging off him and he seemed weak, like a tree without roots.

'Do the doctors know what's wrong with her?' asked Charlie.

Mr Williams shook his head. 'Not everything. She has a broken leg and her neck and back are damaged. The doctors say it might be weeks before they know how serious it is.'

'She'll be OK, Mr Williams. I promise you.' Charlie tried to reassure him.

'I hope you're right, Charlie, I really do.'

In an effort to distract him, Charlie told Mr Williams as much as she knew about Noble Warrior's kidnap. He listened attentively, as if relieved to have something else to think about.

'We had a few small thefts from Cherrydown a couple of years back,' he said. 'I put in the big black gates then and had security cameras installed. The yards have always been padlocked, so it would be very difficult to take a horse, but we had rugs disappear and bits of tack, and then some of the farm machinery went missing. There was one lad who left soon after we put the cameras in and it all stopped after that.'

'Where did he go?' asked Charlie.

'I've no idea,' said Alex Williams. 'It's awful to think there are people out there who are so willing to steal things that aren't theirs, and to steal a horse – well, that's just evil.'

They had reached the doors and Mr Williams pressed the button which released them.

'Now you be careful, Charlie,' he said. 'These could be very dangerous people and I don't want to be worrying about you as well. Let me know if there's anything I can do to help. Good luck!'

Chapter 8

'How's she doing?' asked Bill Bass, as Charlie came back into the waiting room.

'She's trying to be so brave,' said Charlie quietly. 'But Mr Williams says she's hurt her back and her neck. She had a head brace on. I don't even know if she can move or not.'

'These things always look worse than they are,' said Bill. 'Give her a few days and you can come back and visit again.'

'Polly said the truck that spooked Munchkin was grey and blue, just like ours, and she heard banging from the back. I think it was Noddy kicking the sides because he was scared. We've got to find them, Dad. It's not just about getting Noddy back any more: we've got to catch the kidnappers for Polly.'

'In that case,' said her dad, 'we really can't pay any ransom. They'll be off with the money faster than Noble Warrior at top speed. You might get him back, but you'll never see them again.'

Charlie sighed. 'You're right, Dad. And there really isn't a moment to lose. If we're going to find them, we need to do it fast. That policewoman said the best chance of finding Noddy is in the first forty-eight hours. He's already been missing for more than ten. He could be anywhere in the country. Or even France or Ireland by now.'

'Let's get back home then,' said her dad, 'and plan our next move.'

By the time Charlie and Bill got back to Folly Farm, the BBC film footage from the Open Day had arrived.

'They've sent everything they filmed,' explained Harry. 'We can look through it and see if there's a clear shot of either of the men. Then we can take a screengrab and that's our Wanted poster.'

'Do you think we should be that obvious?' said Granny Pam, sweeping into the room in a cape and deerstalker.

'Er, what's with the hat, Granny?' asked Charlie.

'You might well ask,' giggled Larry. 'She's been smoking a pipe too.'

'It helps me to get into CHARACTER, darlings. I thought Miss Marple might be a bit soft for this situation so I'm channelling Sherlock.' Granny Pam pushed a monocle into her right eye and raised her hand to her chin. 'Anyway, my point is this: do we want the kidnappers to know we're on their trail? Or do we want to SURPRISE them?'

'We've got to find them first,' said Larry. 'I've phoned every motorway service station within sixty miles of the farm. None of them have seen a cattle truck today.'

'I'm not surprised,' said Caroline. 'There are

cameras all along the motorways and the thieves know they're driving a stolen vehicle. Using minor roads means they'll be much less likely to be spotted. It'll take them a lot longer to get to wherever they're going, of course.'

'But where *are* they going?' exclaimed Charlie in frustration. 'There must be some way to work it out.'

'Wait a minute . . .' Harry had started scanning through the BBC footage and now paused it, just as the two suspicious men approached Charlie. It was impossible to see their faces, but their hats were in clear view. 'I know that badge!'

He grabbed the *Essex Chronicle* and turned it over to the back page. There was a picture of the cricketer Alastair Cook hitting a ball to the boundary.

'Look!' Harry shouted. 'Look at his helmet!'

The blue helmet had a red shield on the front, with an eagle over three wide swords, one above the other. Harry grabbed the iPad and tapped in 'Essex cricket caps'. He showed Charlie the screen and pointed.

'There!' he yelled triumphantly. 'That's the baseball cap our friend was wearing. It's the T20 badge for Essex Eagles. He must be a cricket fan and that's his home side.'

'Harry, that's brilliant!' Charlie exclaimed, momentarily forgetting that she was angry with her brother.

At the same instant, the phone rang.

'Folly Farm, this is Pamela speaking,' declaimed Granny Pam in her poshest voice. She paused, listening. 'One moment, I'll see if she's available.'

Granny Pam handed the phone to Charlie. 'It's for you.'

Charlie frowned. She wasn't expecting anyone to call. She hoped it wasn't Mr Williams ringing with bad news about Polly. She lifted the phone to her ear.

'Hello?'

'Charlie Bass?' The man's voice at the other end of the phone sounded distorted, as if it was coming down a long tube. Charlie felt her stomach tighten. The kidnappers! She put the call on speakerphone.

'Yes, this is Charlie. Who's calling?'

'We've got your 'orse. You've got our note. We want the million pounds by eight o'clock tonight. No police. No publicity. Just the money.'

Charlie swallowed hard. She needed to stall for time.

'We don't have that much, I'm afraid. We could get you half by tonight if you tell us where to find Noble Warrior, and then I promise we'll pay the rest of it by the end of the week.'

There was silence at the end of the phone. Charlie thought she could hear a horse whinnying in the background. She was sure it was Noble Warrior. 'Please, sir,' she continued. 'He's very sensitive and he needs to be here at home.'

'No.' The distorted voice was firm. 'Half ain't good enough. We want the lot or the deal's off.'

'Wait!' Charlie wanted to keep the man on the phone. She needed more clues as to where they were.

'We ain't playing games, little girl. A million pounds. You'd better get it. Until you do, we've got other means of making 'im pay 'is way.'

The kidnapper hung up. Charlie looked at the phone.

'He was using a voice distorter,' said Granny Pam. 'We used one in a play once. It can give you different accents, even change a male voice to a female one. I think he'd selected DARTH VADER.'

'You can get it as an app now,' Larry said. 'That way you can use it on phone calls. I'm guessing he wasn't stupid enough to leave us his number, but we might as well check.' He picked up the phone to dial 1471. 'No such luck. Number withheld.'

'"We've got other means of making him pay his way",' Charlie repeated. 'What does that mean?'

'They could race him illegally,' Larry suggested. 'If no one knew who he was, the kidnappers could win a load of money.'

'That's if they can make him gallop,' said Harry.

'Yeah, but they don't know how difficult that's going to be,' Larry replied. 'All they know is that they've got the Derby winner and they assume he can beat anything.'

'Let's look at the evidence,' said Charlie. 'The kidnappers might have a connection with Essex. And they might be planning to race Noddy illegally. But how can we be sure?'

Granny Pam shot to her feet. 'I've got it! You know, my darling, that I have contacts ALL over the country? It's what comes of being on tour for most of my life. I've been to every THEE-AH-TER up and down the land and made friends at all of them. Well, one of my very BEST friends lives in Essex – in Chelmsford, in fact. She played Letitia Blacklock to my Miss Marple. Her stage name was Kate Bennett, but we all call her Kitty Poo. She's our "woman on the ground" – we can ask her if there's been anything in the local news about illegal horse racing.'

Granny Pam seized the phone and stabbed at the buttons.

'It's ringing,' she whispered conspiratorially. Then she shrieked, 'Kitty Poo, DARLING! It's Pam. Yes, that was Caroline on *BBC Breakfast* this morning. Wonderful, wasn't she? An absolute natural! Must get her performance skills from me. Ha ha ha! Oh, and by the way, she says Mike Morgan is an absolute DISH in real life. Who knew?'

'Granny!' hissed Charlie. 'Ask her about the illegal racing.'

'Oh, yes, of course,' said Granny Pam. 'Listen, Kitty Poo, we've got a bit of a situation here. Charlie's horse has been KIDNAPPED. No, not the pony, the racehorse. Yes, the one who won the DERBY. Look, we think that he might have been taken to Essex, and that the thieves could be planning to race him illegally. Does that SORT OF THING go on down your way?'

Granny Pam paused as she listened.

'Is that so?' she said. 'And where exactly is that?'

She whipped a notepad from under her cape and scribbled furiously.

'Wonderful, darling. You're a love. Catch up soon and THANK YOU!'

Granny Pam hung up and turned to Charlie.

'You won't believe this. Kitty Poo says that there was an article in the paper this week about an

illegal trap race held every year near Corringham, on the way to Southend-on-Sea. Apparently, it's a BIG DEAL – the winning horse and driver can make a fortune!'

'That's it!' Charlie wanted to dance on the spot she was so excited. 'At the Open Day the kidnappers asked me and Joe if Noddy had ever pulled a cart or a trap! Your friend Kitty has given us the biggest clue of all – now we know where to look!'

Charlie kissed Granny Pam on the cheek. Suddenly she felt as if they were no longer blundering around in the dark. It finally made sense. The kidnappers wanted the ransom money, but, if they couldn't get that, they had a Plan B, which was to win money with Noddy at illegal race meetings. But their greed had been their own undoing, providing the clue that would lead Charlie to Noble Warrior – and justice for Polly.

'We don't have any time to waste,' Charlie said. 'Essex is a long way away. Who's coming?'

Granny Pam was the first to wave her hand in the air. 'I am, naturally. I had a strong fan base in East

132

Anglia, back in the day. I remember a sell-out run at the Mercury Theatre in Colchester. Must've been the early seventies. I was young and free and very much FOOTLOOSE.' Granny Pam started tap-dancing, as if to emphasize the point.

Caroline looked embarrassed. 'Mum, now is not the time for a dance number. I'm happy to drive, but someone needs to stay here to be on hand in case the police come back again.'

'I'll stay,' said Bill. 'The cows will need milking and I can talk to the vet when she comes back to check on Percy. Joe's with him now. I'll go and tell him what's happening.'

'I think Joe will have to come with us,' said Charlie. 'If we do find Noddy, we might need to get him out in a hurry and, if that means riding him, Joe's the only one who can do that.'

Harry and Larry were both keen to come, but started fighting about which one would be more useful.

'I've got karate moves,' said Harry, aiming a kick directly at Larry's head.

'Yeah, well, I've got a cracking right hook,' replied Larry, swinging his fist at Harry's chin. His brother leaned back just in time so that the blow glanced off.

'Boys!' shouted Caroline. 'Neither of you will be coming if you behave like that. This is a rescue mission, not a prize fight.'

Like puppies who had been told off, the boys lowered their heads. If they'd had tails, they would have been between their legs. For the first time that day, Charlie felt sorry for them.

'Well, you have worked hard trying to track down the cattle truck,' she said. 'And you did make the connection between the baseball cap and Essex. And we could need your karate and boxing skills, but it might be an idea to save your moves for the kidnappers.'

Joe came in from the barn.

'Percy's nearly back to his old self,' he said with a smile. 'He's getting hungry and he keeps whinnying for Noddy, which is a good sign. Your dad says he'll keep an eye on him until the vet comes back this evening. He said you wanted to see me?'

Charlie explained how they had worked out where Noble Warrior might be.

'Great sleuthing skills,' said Joe admiringly. 'What do the police think?'

Charlie made a face. 'We haven't told them. They want us to stay put and do nothing, but I *can't*. I'm sure he's there, but the police will only say there's no hard evidence. We have to find Noddy ourselves. When we've done that, we can call them.'

'In that case,' said Joe, 'what are we waiting for?'

Chapter 9

Caroline climbed behind the wheel of her new people carrier. After the Derby win, she had talked about getting a Jaguar XKR, but had settled for the more practical option. Right now, that seemed like a good decision. Granny Pam slid into the passenger seat while Harry, Larry, Charlie and Joe got in the back. Boris hopped in with them and started barking, as if to tell them he was ready for departure.

'Which way?' asked Caroline, when they got to the bottom of the drive.

'Left!' Harry shouted.

'Right!' Larry yelled.

'Shut up!' snarled Harry, putting Larry in a headlock. 'Google Maps says the quickest way is to go left, then head for the A303 and up to the M3.'

'Yeah, well, the TomTom says go right, down to the M27 and then up the A31 and the A3,' retorted Larry, jabbing Harry in the kidneys.

Charlie sighed and looked up from the road map. 'It's a left and then a right and cut across to the A354 up to Salisbury. That'll take us to the A30, through Stockbridge and on to the M3.'

'Thank you,' said Caroline. 'A bit of calm direction under pressure. Just like Kate Richardson-Walsh in the Olympic hockey final. You boys can go all Maddie Hinch when we get there, and terrify the pants off those horrible men, but right now we need a bit of Captain Kate. Well done, Charlie.'

The journey took forever. The 50mph speed limit through the roadworks on the M3 didn't help and the traffic on the M25 was nose to tail. Charlie bit her nails absent-mindedly and kept looking at her watch. It would be nearly dark by the time they got to Essex, and they still had to work out exactly where and when the race meeting was happening. If it was illegal, it would hardly be advertised in the local paper.

Charlie shut her eyes and she must have nodded off for a while because, when she woke up, it was pitch-black.

'Is it dark already?'

'Not yet, sweetheart,' her mother replied. 'We're in a tunnel. We'll be out in a minute and then it's only about another half an hour to Corringham. We should be there by eight o'clock. I reckon we should stop for a bite to eat first, though.'

As much as Charlie didn't want to stop, she knew her mum was right. The search for Noble Warrior was only just beginning. They needed to keep their strength up.

Caroline followed the signs for THURROCK (LAKESIDE) and drove into the biggest shopping complex Charlie had ever seen. There was a grey tower with signs for all the different shops – you could buy clothes, toys, furniture, food, sports gear, carpets, computers, coffee or sandwiches.

'We should've come here with our Derby winnings,' said Harry. 'Think of all the extra computer gear we could've got.'

'I'd have bought a new cricket bat and pads,' said Larry, pointing at a massive sports shop.

'You don't play cricket,' his brother observed.

'Yeah, but that's only because I haven't got any of the kit,' argued Larry. 'If I did, I'd be better than Ben Stokes!'

'Never mind that,' said Charlie. 'I'm starving. We need food and we need Wi-Fi so you can get on that iPad of yours and see if you can find out any more about Corringham. That's where Granny's friend said the races happen.'

Caroline drove towards the first restaurant she could find and pulled up close to the entrance.

'I'd forgotten how much I hate the M25,' she said, as she got out of the car.

'Darling, you should have said,' exclaimed Granny Pam, who was already walking towards the restaurant, her cape billowing behind her. 'I had a walk-out with James Hunt many years ago. He taught me everything he knew. I'd have been ducking and diving between those lanes like an ELECTRIC EEL!'

'Who's James Hunt?' asked Charlie, running to catch up while Boris had a pee against a lamp post.

'Oh, he was a dashing man. The most naturally talented racing driver you've ever seen.' Granny Pam sighed. 'He was quite smitten with me, you know, but I had my career and he had his. It wasn't to be . . . Now, remember, we're travelling UNDERCOVER – we don't want the kidnappers to know that we're coming. Leave the talking to me.'

Granny Pam swung the front of her cape across her face as she went inside and hurried over to a waitress, grabbing a menu en route.

'We need a table in the corner where no one can see us.' She pointed at the menu as she issued her order. 'Three of your special pizzas, three of those pastas and a bottle of water. Fast as you can, my girl!'

The waitress looked at Charlie and down at Boris.

'I'm sorry, no dogs.'

Granny Pam stepped between them.

'Don't touch the dog,' she said in a low voice. 'He has to be by her side at all times. Assistance dog, you see. Essential and LETHAL.'

'Lethal?' exclaimed the waitress in alarm.

'Not lethal,' interrupted Charlie, thinking quickly. '*Legal*. He's a legally registered assistance dog.'

The waitress didn't seem all that convinced, but still led them towards a table in the corner.

Charlie looked quizzically at her mother.

'Don't pay any attention,' said Caroline. 'Mum used to do this all the time when I was young and it was excruciatingly embarrassing. It's best to ignore her until she comes to her senses.'

Harry and Larry fell through the door behind Joe, pushing and shoving each other as they crossed the restaurant floor. Caroline sat them on opposite sides of the table so they had to stop fighting. Larry aimed a final kick at Harry, but his leg couldn't quite reach.

'Can you get on the Wi-Fi, Larry?' asked Charlie, trying to distract him. 'See what you can find about illegal racing nearby.'

Larry tapped his finger on the screen.

'Wow!' he exclaimed. 'It's come up with loads of results straight away. This forum looks interesting . . .'

He slid the iPad over to Charlie so that she could see what he had found.

'"Calling all racers,"' read Charlie. '"Gather ye at the Manor Way for a feast fit for a king." Then there are some numbers. What does it mean?'

'Could be a code,' said Granny Pam, putting her monocle to her eye. 'Let me see.' She grabbed the iPad and stared at the screen. 'See the insignia in the corner, Watson? The CHARIOT!'

'It's Charlie, Granny Pam. Who's Watson?'

Granny Pam shook her head. 'Sorry, got carried

away for a moment there. Back in the present, stay in the present. LOOK OUT! Interloper approaching!'

'Mother, stop being so dramatic. It's just the waitress.' Caroline smiled at the poor girl, who was clearly sweating. She put the pizzas and pasta down quickly, looking nervously under the table at Boris, and hurried back to the kitchen.

'That's what I'm talking about,' beamed Harry, slurping up a forkful of spaghetti bolognese. Across the table, Larry shoved half a pizza into his mouth in one go.

Joe eyed the food warily.

'Is everything OK, Joe?' asked Caroline.

'Sorry, I don't mean to be fussy. It looks a bit . . . heavy, that's all.'

'We're carb-loading,' Granny Pam snapped back. 'You'll need ALL the energy you can get for tonight.'

'Oh, how silly of me,' said Caroline. 'I know you're keeping an eye on your racing weight.' She waved the waitress over. 'Could we have a green salad as well, please, and two more of those pizzas? Thank you.'

The waitress ran away again.

'I've cracked it!' declared Granny Pam, putting the iPad down. 'The numbers are a grid reference and *this* is the date. It's today!'

Granny Pam handed the iPad back to Larry and he copied the grid reference on to another site as the waitress reappeared with the extra food.

'It looks as if they're meeting in Springhouse Lane,' said Larry. 'It's just off the dual carriageway near Corringham. King of the Road is what they call the meeting that they hold every year. Weird name for a horse race.'

The waitress gasped.

'What is it?' asked Charlie.

'King of the Road – is that what you said?' replied the waitress.

'Yes, what of it?' Granny Pam shot back.

'Granny,' said Charlie sharply. 'No need to be rude.'

'Please,' Caroline said gently, 'do go on.'

'It's only that it's quite rough,' the waitress said.

'What do you mean, "rough"?' Caroline asked.

'Well, the police, they're always trying to get it stopped, but they can't. The men who run it ain't scared of no one. Don't matter to them if they cause an accident or if them 'orses get 'urt. They don't care. They just wanna win the money. There's a big pot, you see, for the 'orse that wins.'

'What do you mean, "cause an accident"?' asked Charlie.

The waitress grimaced. 'They start with knockout rounds in the field next to Springhouse Lane, just off the dual carriageway. I saw it once, but it made me feel really sad, the way they battered those poor 'orses. They make 'em gallop flat out, pulling a little carriage behind 'em, and then the four fastest ones are lined up on the dual carriageway and they race 'em till they drop. The last one left standing is the winner. It's brutal.'

Charlie gasped in horror. It was even worse than she'd thought.

'What about the cars? How do they stop the traffic?' she asked.

'Sometimes they use a coupla cars or vans to go slow and stop other cars getting past so the 'orses 'ave a clear run, but sometimes they don't bother and the 'orses just have to go through the traffic. The blokes that organize it, they don't care.' The

146

waitress shook her head, as she backed away from the table. 'Just be careful, that's all I'm saying.'

Charlie looked around the table. Joe was as white as a sheet. Caroline was chewing the insides of her cheek. Granny Pam had her head bowed. Even Harry and Larry had fallen silent. None of them could understand how people could treat horses so cruelly.

Charlie swallowed hard. 'If what she says is true, there's no time to lose: we've got to save Noddy before they start the racing. His legs will never stand galloping on a road. It could ruin him forever.'

Everyone nodded. They knew how much was at stake.

'Ve shall heff to be clever and clandestine,' Granny Pam said, in a strange accent.

'Clandestine?' Charlie didn't understand.

'Stealthy, secretive, crafty,' Caroline explained. 'And, if that's the case, Mother, you can't go dressed like that. You'll stand out a mile. Besides, you've got bolognese all over the cape.'

'Worry not, daughter dear,' replied Granny Pam. 'I have the PERFECT disguise for this evening's pursuit...'

Chapter 10

While Granny Pam disappeared into the loo to change, Charlie took the opportunity to share her plan for the evening.

'It sounds as if it could be dangerous tonight, so I want us all to work in pairs for safety and so that no one gets lost. Mum, you take Granny Pam. Harry and Larry, you two had best stay together. Joe, you come with me and Boris. We'll look at the horses to see if we can find Noddy. Mum, you look for the

149

cattle truck, and you two,' she looked from Harry to Larry, 'you might be needed to cause a distraction.'

Larry had finished his second pizza and was getting bored. He slid down to reach under the table and kicked Harry on the ankle. Harry tried to grab his foot and the table rocked.

'Seriously?!' Charlie said furiously. 'Would you two just knock it off for one minute. If you want to help – and I mean *really* help – it would be a good idea to just grow up a bit!'

'Ooh!' Harry put on a voice. 'Hark at our little sister telling us what to do. Yes, miss, of course, miss, anything you want, miss.'

Charlie felt tears start to prick the surface of her eyes. She was trying so hard not to let her anger get the better of her, but taking on her brothers was exhausting.

'OW!' Harry's head bent to one side and his hand shot up to his ear. 'Arghh, get off!'

Granny Pam had returned from the loo transformed. Her hair was now flowing over her shoulders and she had a purple headscarf worn as a bandana round her forehead and tied so that the ends fell down her back. She had on a long skirt, black boots and a pale blue off-the-shoulder top. The sleeves were wide and, when she moved, the material billowed softly around her. She was pinching Harry's ear and twisting it.

'Granny, let go! That hurts!'

'Pull yourself together, boy. If you can't behave, we'll leave you and your useless brother here for the night. You can help WASH UP in the kitchen.'

'All right, all right!' Harry winced with pain. 'We'll be good. I promise!'

Granny Pam released her grip and leaned forward.

'You'd BETTER keep that promise or, believe me, you won't have an ear to hear me with.'

Charlie looked from Harry, his eyes wide with fear, to Granny Pam, who winked at her.

'I know you believe in patience and teamwork,' Granny Pam whispered conspiratorially, 'but sometimes, with boys, a bit of brute force is the only way.'

The waitress came to clear their table and looked sideways at Granny Pam in confusion. She hesitated. Some of the dirty plates were next to Boris, who was sitting on the bench alongside Charlie. Granny Pam beamed.

'Don't be scared,' said Granny Pam. 'That other woman – the one in the RIDICULOUS cape – she makes things up. This is the kindest dog in the world. Give him a pat. He won't bite you!'

The waitress reached out and briefly ruffled the smooth hair on top of Boris's head.

'I'm sure 'e's very nice,' she said and looked back to Granny Pam. 'But could you tell the other lady that she's left 'er cape and 'er 'at in the ladies' loo? Thanks.'

She cleared the rest of the plates and, as she carried them back to the kitchen, Caroline left enough money to cover the bill plus a large tip. The waitress deserved it for the information she had given them.

The Basses left the restaurant as quickly as they could, apart from Granny Pam, who stopped off at every table to chat to people.

'The pepperoni pizza is very good,' Charlie heard her comment to one family. 'I'd recommend the spaghetti bolognese,' she suggested to another.

'Make sure you talk to each other and don't spend all evening staring at THOSE,' she said loudly to a couple who were both checking their mobile phones. 'It's the quickest way to ruin a relationship.'

'Granny!' hissed Charlie, hustling her towards the door. 'Come on, we've got to go.'

'Probably worth popping into that sports shop,' said Granny Pam, pointing. 'You boys should get yourself a pair of those Essex Eagles baseball caps. They'll help you BLEND IN.'

'You know what, Mother?' said Caroline. 'Sometimes – just sometimes – you do have some sensible ideas.' Caroline beckoned to the boys and led them across the car park.

'You've been very quiet, Joe,' said Charlie. 'Are you OK?'

'I'm just thinking,' he said, twisting his fingers anxiously. 'If we do find Noddy, how will we get him home? The cattle truck is no good in the dark and he won't fit in here.'

He gestured to the car, which was big enough for the six of them and Boris, but clearly wouldn't take a fully grown horse.

'I know,' replied Charlie. 'I've been worrying about that too. But first we've got to find him and stop the kidnappers running him on the road. We'll work out the next move when we have to.'

The boys returned with their baseball caps pulled low over their heads. Harry had squeezed the peak of his cap so that it folded in the middle and didn't look brand-new. Larry had jumped up and down on his, just to make sure.

Caroline drove them out of the shopping centre and back on to the dual carriageway. She followed the A13 until they reached the turn for Corringham. The sun was dipping in the sky behind them and the clouds were turning pale pink.

'The field is off to the right over there,' said Larry, staring at the map on his iPad. 'Looks like you have to turn off the main road here on the left and then double back on yourself. Straight over those traffic lights and down that lane.'

Caroline drove slowly down the single-track road bordered by fields filled with short yellow wheat stubble. About a mile down the road there was a turning with a sign saying No Public Right of Way. The metal gate that had acted as a barrier was swinging open, the chain that had kept it locked dangling down.

Granny Pam opened her window. She stuck her head out and listened.

'I can hear people shouting. Sounds like a big crowd. And I'm sure I heard a horse whinnying.'

'Mum.' Charlie's voice was urgent. 'Keep driving. We need to park the car somewhere out of sight. We'll be better off walking the rest of the way. We mustn't do anything to draw attention to ourselves. If the kidnappers recognize us, who knows what they might do!'

Caroline drove on for half a mile until they came to a farm and parked behind a hedge opposite the drive. Everyone in the car fell silent. Charlie felt a fluttering in her stomach. It was like the sensation she'd had before the Derby, but then she'd had a clear plan, worked out well in advance. This time they were improvising, and Charlie didn't like it.

'BUTTERFLIES!' exclaimed Granny Pam suddenly, turning round from the passenger seat to look at all of them. 'It's just a sign of adrenalin. I used to get them all the time right before I went on stage. I'd have worried if I *hadn't* felt like that. You have to use it. Harness the energy and the awareness they create. Be alert, be sharp and look out for each other.'

'Remember to stay in your pairs,' Charlie said. 'Joe and I will look for Noddy. Mum and Granny Pam, you're trying to find the cattle truck, in case we need a quick getaway. Harry and Larry, you see if you can blend in and pick up any information that might help us.'

But, while Charlie had chosen the quiet, gentle approach, Granny Pam was clearly ready for all-out war.

'We have a horse to find and a pair of mean-spirited men to bring down. Are we READY?'

Granny Pam delivered her rousing call as if standing on stage. The car resounded with her voice.

'I said, ARE WE READY?'

Charlie and her brothers nodded. Joe nodded. Caroline in the driver's seat nodded. Even Boris joined in.

'READY!' they shouted as one.

They split into their pairs and made their way across the field. Charlie was thinking about all the things that might happen. What if they found Noddy too late and he'd already been injured? What if the kidnappers found *them* and kidnapped the family too? What if they were in the wrong place entirely?

'My head is so full that it's starting to hurt,' she confided to Joe.

'Try not to think too much,' he replied. 'I know it's difficult, but see if you can feel your feet, listen to the sound of the stubble as you walk through it, sense the wind, look at the sky changing colour. I do it when I'm nervous before a race and it makes me calmer.'

Charlie walked on in silence, trying to follow Joe's advice. She wiggled her toes and became aware of her legs and her arms. She listened to the crunch of her footsteps landing on the shaven wheat stalks and she felt the temperature start to drop as the sun was setting. As they got closer, she could smell burning and noticed the plume of smoke coming from a large bonfire. She could hear music and the whoops of people dancing.

People were gathered round the fire, some of them chatting, some eating, some holding hands. Children with bare feet and grubby faces were running around. One section of the crowd was watching a man with no shirt on. His head was shorn, but his grey beard gave away his age. He had a heavy metal chain looped around his body and was wiggling and writhing, trying to free himself. Another man was looking at a watch and counting down.

'Come on, Johnny, you can do it!' shouted a younger man in jeans and a T-shirt.

'Thirty seconds left,' said the man with the watch.

Johnny bent his right shoulder towards his chest and the chain moved. He gritted his teeth and flinched as his shoulder came closer to his chin and clicked. The chain slipped over his shoulder and his arm was free. He flinched again as he moved his shoulder back and it clicked into place. Then he used his free hand to pull the chain down until he stood with it at his feet. He raised his arms above his head and grinned. There was a huge cheer from the crowd.

'No one keeps Johnny in chains!' he cried.

'Success, ladies and gents, with ten seconds to spare. Pay up,' said the man with the watch.

'Told you he'd do it.' The younger man who had been cheering on Johnny turned to the man next to him. 'He's over sixty and still stronger than anyone else here. That's fifty quid you owe me.'

Charlie glanced at Joe and urged him with her eyes to shadow her as she moved closer to the group. Boris was at her heels and, when she stopped, he sniffed the air. Then he growled. He was looking at the man who had lost the bet.

'Joe, it's him!' Charlie gasped. 'The whispering man from the Open Day! We're in the right place. Noddy must be here too!'

Charlie's heart was thumping so hard she was worried the whispering man would hear it from where he was standing. Adrenalin coursed through her veins, banishing fear and making her feel exhilarated.

The whispering man looked up and turned his head towards them. As he did so, Charlie grabbed Joe's arm and whirled him round as if they were dancing.

'Quick!' she said. 'Keep moving. We've got to find Noddy before that man sees us.'

Just beyond the bonfire, a group of women were laughing. They were wearing exactly the sort of brightly coloured clothes that Granny Pam had put on. A couple of dogs that looked like greyhounds with long hair roamed around them, sniffing the ground and picking up scraps of food. One of them lifted his head and looked at Boris, who leaned into Charlie's leg for protection.

'It's OK, fella. He won't eat you.' Charlie reached down to reassure Boris and, sure enough, the dog walked past, ignoring him.

'Where are they keeping all the horses?' Charlie muttered to herself. 'They must be close.'

The women were laughing even louder now. One of them had her back to Charlie, but was clearly telling them a funny story. The ends of a purple scarf trailed down past her shoulders and her voice was heavily accented. Boris darted forward, wagging his tail.

'Boris, don't!' hissed Charlie, but it was too late. Boris ran to the woman and jumped up at her skirt.

'Oh, vot a SVEET little dog!' the woman said, as she turned towards Charlie. 'Ees it yars?'

Charlie tried to keep the shock off her face. Granny Pam was staring straight at her, behaving as if she'd never met Charlie in her life!

'I vas just telling a little story about my little pooch who ate ALL za money I von at zee last King ov za Road!' Granny Pam turned

back towards her new friends. 'Vot time vill the racing begin today?' she asked.

'As soon as the sun goes below the horizon,' said the woman closest to Granny Pam. 'They're getting the horses ready for the knockout stage soon and then they'll head up to the dual carriageway.'

'Not long zen. Not long at all.' Granny Pam looked at Charlie again. 'You had better take your SVEET little dog to see za horses. Ver are zey?'

The woman pointed to the next field. Charlie and Joe hurried towards a small gap in the hedge that stood between them.

'What's Granny Pam doing?' said Charlie. 'She's supposed to be looking for the cattle truck with Mum!'

Joe grinned. 'She's doing what she does best,' he replied. 'Making sure she's the centre of attention! And it worked, didn't it? Now we know where we're going.'

Ducking through the gap in the hedge, Charlie and Joe found a very different scene. There were no groups of laughing people here, no sideshows or food or music. The field was full of horses tethered to posts so that they could move in a circle but not stray any further. One skewbald horse with long hair on the bottoms of its legs was pawing at the ground. It looked hungry.

About twelve small contraptions with wheels were lined up on the far side of the field. A man was harnessing a horse to one of them. Long white bars went on either side of the horse and were attached by a strap across its chest. There were long reins on the horse's bridle that passed back to the seat of the carriage, which was like a tiny little chariot, with a low-slung seat for the driver.

'Charlie, look!' Joe pointed towards the hedge where there were a few vehicles parked. Right in the middle was a familiar grey-and-blue shape. 'It's the cattle truck!'

Suddenly from inside the truck came the most almighty bang. Then another, and another. A man jumped out of the front and banged a stick on the side.

'Shut up, I told you!' he shouted, banging the

stick louder. 'I'll come in there and hit you with this if you don't stop kicking, you stupid horse.'

The man was clearly angry, but all the time he was grinning as if someone had just told him a joke.

'It's the other man who came to the Open Day,' murmured Joe. 'Noddy must still be in the truck.'

Charlie felt her heart leap. 'We've found him!'

Chapter 11

Charlie wanted to punch the grinning man right in his toothy mouth. She felt more anger and aggression than at any time in her life. How dare he and that stupid, whispering creep take her horse? How dare they separate him from Percy and steal their cattle truck? How dare they put her friend Polly in hospital with serious injuries?

Charlie's eyes were blazing and, when she looked

down at her hands, she saw they were balled into fists. She was ready for a fight. She could see Joe's lips moving, but she couldn't hear what he was saying. The blood was throbbing so much in her ears that nothing was getting through.

Joe put his hand on Charlie's arm and she jumped as if he'd burned her.

He stood in front of her and put his hands on her shoulders. 'Listen to me, Charlie! We can't take them on in a fight. We won't win.'

Charlie took a deep breath.

'You're right, Joe. I know you're right. Let's find the others and work out what we *can* do.'

As they turned to go back, though, Caroline popped her head through the gap in the hedge.

'What's happening?' she asked. 'Have you found him?'

'Mum, he's in the truck.' Charlie gestured towards the cattle truck. 'He's scared and the horrible, grinning man who was at the Open Day keeps bashing the side and that's making Noddy even more frantic. We've got to get him out!'

The banging from the cattle truck started again and, as they looked towards the noise, the whispering man joined his grinning friend.

Suddenly Boris started wagging his tail and jumping up at Charlie's side. He ran towards the hedge and back again. Through the gap came Harry and Larry. Harry's right eye was swollen and he had blood coming from his nose. He held his left hand up to his face and limped towards them. Larry was helping him.

'What have you been up to now?' exclaimed Caroline. 'Larry, how could you do this to your brother?'

'It wasn't me!' Larry looked horrified. 'Some boys by the bonfire started picking on me, and Harry jumped in to defend me. They held him down. I couldn't do anything about it.'

Harry tried to speak, but his mouth wouldn't open properly. Caroline pulled out a tissue and started cleaning his face. Harry winced.

'Keep still!' said Caroline, as she kept dabbing his nose, his cheek and his top lip. 'We need to

get you some ice for your eye. It's closing up.'

'That waitress was right when she said it was a rough crowd,' said Joe. 'We need to be careful here.'

Seeing Harry hurt reminded Charlie of Polly, lying in a hospital bed, not knowing whether she would ever walk again. But she knew she must think logically and calmly. Pure rage wouldn't get her anywhere.

'Did you see a list of names for the races?' Charlie asked.

'Yeah,' answered Larry. 'I saw them chalked up on a betting board. There are ten horses to begin with and they go head-to-head to decide which ones go into the final race. I guess they have to narrow it down because it's not safe to gallop ten horses on the road.'

'They're going to gallop these horses on a tarmac dual carriageway and they might not even stop the traffic to do it,' said Charlie passionately. 'I don't think they care about safety.'

Across the field, the first of the chariots had been attached to a horse, and a man in tracksuit bottoms with no shirt on had climbed into the seat. His legs were out in front of him, either side of the horse's flanks. He took the reins in his hand and shouted at the horse to move forward, flicking a long whip as he did so. The horse started to trot and then canter.

'G'wan, g'wan, you miserable mule!' The man cracked the whip hard across the horse's back and then towards its head. The horse picked up speed as the man yanked on the reins to make it turn to the right.

Joe and Charlie both winced.

'If this is the warm-up, what will they be like in the race itself? It's horrifying.' Joe was now the one to be outraged. 'We have to stop it.'

'I can't watch.' As Charlie turned away, she saw the group of colourfully dressed women making their way towards them. At the head of the group was Granny Pam. Charlie reached down to grab Boris's collar before he could run forward to greet her.

'Vot, vot! Ready to trot?' asked Granny Pam. 'Ze races are about to start!'

The crowd was swelling as women, men and children made their way through the gap in the hedge and into the field with the chariots. Another horse had been harnessed up and was cantering round the field, and two more were being prepared. All were much more heavily built than Noble Warrior. Most of them had shaved manes, but the hair on their bodies was thick, especially towards the bottom of their legs, where they had long tufts hanging down towards their feet. They had thicker bones than a thoroughbred and would be less likely to be injured by galloping on a road, but it would still be a horrible experience for them.

Charlie looked back to find Granny Pam, but she had disappeared into the crowd.

'Hello, my little friend, what are you doing here?'

Charlie felt a presence by her side and a voice that sounded familiar. As she turned to take a proper look, she saw jet-black hair, a hooked nose and a gap-toothed smile.

'You're here!'

Charlie flung her arms round the fortune-teller. She had met the descendant of Gypsy Rose Lee in the middle of Epsom Downs on Derby Day. When the fortune-teller had predicted a magical day for Charlie, Charlie had repaid her by telling her that Noble Warrior was the horse to bet on. 'You were right! We did win the Derby!'

'Oh, don't you worry, my little friend. I know you did. I got this as a present to myself afterwards.' She patted her skirt, a beautiful silk patchwork of gold and green. 'I even picked your colours. Foreteller Ava will never forget the girl with the golden touch.'

Ava paused and stared into Charlie's eyes.

'Now, my child, you'd better tell me what you're doing here. I can see by your face that something is wrong. What is it?'

Charlie hesitated. She wasn't sure whether Ava would help her or if the men who took Noble Warrior were friends of hers. The fortune-teller seemed to sense her suspicion.

'You can trust me, my little one. Foreteller Ava never forgets a friend who has done her a good deed. You told me to back your horse and I made a very nice sum that day. I will do anything to repay you.'

Charlie quickly filled her in on what had happened the night before at Folly Farm and how they had come to Essex in the hope of finding Noble Warrior.

'He's in there,' she said, gesturing towards the cattle truck. 'I have a plan to set him free, but I don't know if the crowd is going to like it.'

Ava nodded. 'Let me talk to some of my friends. I'll see what can be done.' She slipped back through the hedge and disappeared.

'Look!' said Harry, still clutching his bloody nose.

The whispering man and his grinning friend were pulling down the back ramp of the cattle truck, ready to lead Noble Warrior out.

'What are we going to do?' asked Caroline. 'Call the police?'

Charlie's pulse was pounding. Within minutes, Noddy would be tied up to a chariot and racing. There was no point in calling the police. They would never get here in time.

'Too late for that. We're going to have to save him ourselves. We need to work as a team,' Charlie said, gesturing for Harry, Larry, Caroline and Joe to huddle in to listen to her plan, like the Great Britain hockey team just before the start of the Olympic final.

'Right. Once the kidnappers have got Noddy out, Harry and Larry, I need you to cause that diversion we talked about. I don't care what you do – just make sure the whole crowd is looking at you. Mum, when everyone's distracted, you jump into the truck. If the kidnappers think someone is stealing it, they'll follow you. Then Joe and I will grab Noddy. Timing is everything, so you need to wait for the signal and then we all move together. Got it?' Charlie finished her directions.

'Righto, captain!' said Larry.

For a moment, Charlie thought her brother was making fun of her again, but he wasn't. His face was deadly serious. Everyone understood their role and they were all ready to help. Charlie felt a surge of pride in her family. This was their chance to save Noble Warrior and they all knew it would probably be their only one.

The kidnappers had moved the last chariot closer to the cattle truck.

'We haven't got long,' Charlie whispered urgently. She still had one person she needed to talk to and the best team member to help her with *that* mission was right by her feet. 'Go on, boy – go and find Granny Pam! Find her!'

Boris sniffed the air for a second and then darted forward, his tail wagging so hard it seemed to act as a propeller. Charlie ran behind him and, thirty seconds later, Boris was jumping up at the skirt of Granny Pam.

'I'm so sorry, madam,' said Charlie, bending down to grab his collar. 'My dog has a mind of his own.'

'Don't vorry. He is a pretty little thing,' replied Granny Pam, leaning down to pat his head.

In the five seconds that their heads were together, bent over Boris, Charlie gave the final instructions she needed to deliver. As Granny Pam stood up, she smiled and spread her arms.

'Let zee GAMES begin!'

Chapter 12

The field was now full of activity. Horses were galloping in different directions, their drivers trying to turn them at high speed. One chariot flipped over and a group of men ran forward to help the driver set it upright again. The two kidnappers had disappeared inside the cattle truck, and Charlie could hear shouting and kicking from inside. She and Joe kept their distance, worried that they might be recognized.

The kidnappers were backing Noble Warrior down the ramp. He was sweating and showing the whites of his eyes. Every time he tried to throw his head in the air, the grinning man tugged down on a rope. Charlie saw that he had tied the short rope in a loop round Noble Warrior's top lip to make a twitch and was holding a stick that he could twist to make the rope tighter. She'd seen the device before, but only used sparingly and gently to calm a horse down if its coat was being clipped. The pain seemed to numb Noble Warrior into complete submission. They led him towards the chariot and backed him into the harness.

'Clip him in,' said the grinning man, as his partner attached the straps that would fix Noble Warrior into place.

As he threw the strap across his back, Noble Warrior lashed out with his back legs and the whispering man fell over.

'You idiot, Luca!' shouted the grinning man, as he jabbed down on the stick and twisted it tighter. 'I told you we should 'ave taken the stupid pony too.'

'I thought that was just a story to get the papers interested,' replied Luca. 'I didn't realize this one really was crazy.'

'Come on, boys,' muttered Charlie. 'We need to get going.'

Right on cue, a loud yell rang out. At the far end of the field, a circle had formed round two figures who were fighting each other. It was Harry and Larry. Granny Pam had given the boys a crash course in stage combat, showing them how to make a fake fight look convincing. Larry was dancing around his brother, pretending to throw punches, while Harry flung his head back as if he had been hit. Red liquid started to pour from the corner of his mouth. Charlie grinned. No one watching would know that Harry had bitten down on a capsule of fake blood slipped to him by Granny Pam. It looked completely real. Everyone had turned to watch, led by Granny Pam, who was goading the boys and shouting her encouragement.

It was time for Phase Two of the plan.

Using the cattle truck as cover, Caroline, Joe and

Charlie made their way carefully towards the chariot. As they reached the back ramp, Charlie gave the second signal.

'Go on, Boris, go!'

Boris ran forward, barking at the grinning man who was holding Noble Warrior's head. He nipped at his heels and grabbed the back of his trouser leg, pulling as hard as he could. At the same time, Caroline jumped into the cattle truck's cab. She found the key in the ignition and turned it. The engine rumbled loudly as it started to roll forward.

'Oi! Stop there!'

Luca had got back to his feet and was trying to sound the alarm, but he still couldn't raise his voice above a whisper. He chased after the truck, waving.

Meanwhile, the grinning man was busy trying to deal with Boris. He kicked at him, but couldn't free his leg without letting go of the twitch he had put around Noble Warrior's muzzle.

Noble Warrior threw back his head and then reared, pulling the chariot up into the air. As his front legs came down, they caught the grinning man on the side of his head. He fell to the ground, knocked out cold, and Boris jumped on to his chest, growling.

'Good boy!' said Charlie. 'You keep him there.'

Joe went straight to Noble Warrior's head to release the twitch, which was dangling from his top lip.

'You poor lad, you don't need that any more.' Joe was speaking softly, cradling Noble Warrior's head in his arms. 'I'm so sorry, my boy. You don't deserve this. It's OK. You're safe now. I promise you're safe now.'

Charlie moved fast to undo the clips and detach Noble Warrior from the harness.

'You'd better get him out of here before our friend wakes up.' She gestured towards the grinning man, who was starting to stir, and gave Joe a leg-up on to Noble Warrior's back.

'Good boy, Noddy,' she said, giving him a kiss on the nose. 'Now get out of here.'

She looked up at Joe. 'Don't stop for anyone. I'll text you when it's safe to come back.'

Joe grabbed the reins, which were far too long,
and gave Noble Warrior a gentle squeeze on the
tummy. He took off at a gallop, thundered across
the field and jumped the hedge. In less than a
minute, he was out of sight. The crowd who had
been watching Harry and Larry fighting all turned
round.

'Who was that? Pegasus?' exclaimed one man.

'What price is he for King of the Road?' asked
another.

Their clamour was interrupted by a rumble of a different kind.

Like an avalanche moving towards them, a grey-and-blue cattle truck thundered slowly but surely down the field, its ramp dragging behind it. Caroline sat at the wheel, beeping the horn. Alongside the truck, a man was running and jumping up at the passenger door, but he couldn't get a grip and kept falling back. He looked like a demented kangaroo.

As he got closer, his whispering voice could finally be heard.

'Stop, thief! She's trying to steal my truck!'

Most of the onlookers scattered in panic, but one had her wits about her. Granny Pam moved deftly to one side, stuck out her right foot and in one smooth move brought the whispering man crashing to the ground. She sat heavily on his stomach, squeezing the wind from his chest.

'I don't think that truck is yours to be claiming, young man. And, if it's a THIEF you're after, you should just look in the mirror.'

She produced a pair of handcuffs and a set of leg shackles from beneath her long skirts. 'These should do the trick,' she said, as she tossed the leg shackles to Larry and attached the handcuffs herself.

'Er, Granny,' murmured Larry. 'Your accent! I think you've blown your cover.'

Granny Pam looked up to find herself faced by the crowd of women.

'Sorry, darlings,' she beamed at her colourfully dressed friends. 'It's true that I'm not quite what I seemed to be, but this man stole my granddaughter's horse. He HAD to be stopped.'

For a moment, the women stood stony-faced. Then they started whooping and cheering.

Granny Pam leaped to her feet and bowed as if taking a curtain call.

'I haven't had such a standing ovation since I gave my Lady Bracknell,' she beamed. 'STILL got it, boys. STILL got it.'

Further up the field, Boris had his front paws on the grinning man's chest and was growling with the ferocity of a dog four times his size. Charlie grabbed the leather straps from the chariot and started tying them round the man's legs to prevent him running away, but he suddenly sat up, swiping Boris aside and grabbing Charlie's arm.

'You've made a big mistake, little lady,' he hissed into her face. 'Meet my friends.'

Charlie looked round in horror. There were at least twenty men in a circle around her. They either had vests on or were completely bare-chested, so she could see their muscles.

'Well done, lads, just in time,' said the grinning man. 'This pathetic l'il girl was trying to tie me up. She's stolen me 'orse and now she's trying to make a fool of me. You know what to do.'

'They do indeed,' said a female voice from behind them. 'But these are my friends, not yours. Get to it, boys.'

The men stepped forward and lifted the grinning man to his feet. Then they continued to wrap the leather straps round his legs, up his body, all the way to his neck. For the first time since she had met him, Charlie noticed that his grin had disappeared.

'I told you I wouldn't let you down,' said the female voice again. It was Ava! 'Now let's take him back to his good-for-nothing pal and we'll work out what to do with the pair of them.'

Charlie and Boris led the group down the field with the men carrying the kidnapper, now wrapped up like a mummy, above their heads until they dropped him next to Luca, the whispering man. The crowd, which had seemed so intimidating when they had first arrived, started to clap and cheer, and Johnny, the man they'd seen breaking himself out of chains, lifted Charlie up and swung her round.

Charlie took a massive intake of breath and let it out slowly. Then she smiled. It had worked. Her plan had actually worked! She shook her head to relieve the slight feeling of dizziness. She knew she had to say something.

'Thank you all so much for your help. These two men stole my horse. They beat him and scared him and they were trying to bully him into racing against your horses. This isn't the way to treat a horse or any other animal.' Charlie gestured at the chariots and their drivers. 'You don't need to be cruel. You don't need those long whips and you certainly don't need to gallop on the main road. I understand racing and I know what you love about it, but it doesn't have to be like this.'

Ava moved forward and took her hand.

'She's right, lads. We ought to be thinking to the future and not always behaving like we did in the past. We've always been close to our animals, working together to survive, and we should respect them and cherish them because of that.'

A few of the older men started to grumble, but the young children looked eager and interested. However, their discussion was interrupted by the sound of sirens.

'It's the rozzers!' shouted the man who'd been chalking up the betting on a blackboard. 'Scram!'

The crowd scattered in all directions and the drivers with their chariots trotted away down the lanes. By the time a police car with lights flashing and sirens blaring screeched into the field, only

Charlie, Caroline, Granny Pam, Harry, Larry and Ava were left, along with the two kidnappers.

The front doors of the car opened. Chief Inspector Bronks got out of the passenger side and her brother, Sergeant Bronks, got out of the driver's side.

'I told you it was no right turn at those lights!' shouted the Chief Inspector.

'We're in a police car, you fool. We can do what we like!'

'Don't you talk to me like that. I'm your superior officer!'

'You're also my sister, more's the pity, and if I can't tell you you're off your rocker then nobody can.'

Bill Bass slowly got out of the back of the car. Caroline ran forward to hug him.

'Darling! What on earth are you doing here?'

'These two came back to the farm a couple of hours after you'd left. I told them what you'd all worked out about Essex and the illegal racing. They jumped back in the car with me and roared straight over here. I've never driven so fast in my life,' said Bill, rubbing his ears. 'They never stop talking either. They bicker more than Harry and Larry!'

Chief Inspector Bronks surveyed the scene.

'Where's the horse?' she asked, looking confused.

'Joe rode him away,' replied Charlie. 'I'll tell him it's safe to come back.' She borrowed Larry's phone and sent Joe a text:

Coast clear. Police here.

'I don't know how we're going to get Noddy home, though,' added Charlie. 'We can't use the cattle truck because it's got no headlights.'

'Don't worry,' said Bill. 'I called Alex Williams from the car. He's sending his horsebox. It won't be far behind us.'

'Thanks, Dad. Did he say how Polly was doing?'

'No change yet. But when she hears we've found Noddy, that'll cheer her up.' Bill patted his daughter on the head. 'And well done, my love. I'm proud of you. I'm proud of all of you.'

Charlie hugged her father.

'Where are the boys?' asked Bill.

'I've no idea,' replied Charlie. 'They were here a second ago.'

'They're in the police car,' said Granny Pam. She saw the look of horror on Bill's face and quickly added, 'Don't worry, they're not going to do anything BAD. I told them there'd be a first-aid kit in there.'

Meanwhile, Chief Inspector Bronks was staring down at the two men on the ground.

'Luca Cunningham and Lee McGregor, I am arresting you for breaking and entering private property, robbery, kidnapping of a horse and causing grievous bodily harm by dangerous driving. You're both going to prison for a very long time.'

Charlie didn't stay to listen. She could see Noble Warrior and Joe approaching across the field. She ran up to them and stroked Noddy's face tenderly.

'How is he?' she asked.

'He's a bit shaken up,' said Joe, 'but I can't find any serious damage. A few cuts and bruises where he's been kicking, but he hasn't broken any bones. I took him down to the water and bathed his legs in the sea. That should have done him good – and maybe he's tougher than he looks.'

Joe patted Noble Warrior's neck while Charlie kissed him on the side of the nose. 'You'll be back home soon, my boy. Back with Percy and safe in your barn.'

Noble Warrior pricked his ears and whickered softly.

Relief flooded through Charlie and she was

suddenly overcome with exhaustion. It felt like her whole body had been tensed up ever since the moment that morning when they had discovered Noble Warrior was missing. Now she felt like she could sleep for a week. She wanted to talk to Joe about his job offer in Ireland and she was desperate to see Polly, but both would have to wait.

'Well, I should be moving on,' said Ava. 'It's a long walk back to Corringham.'

'Why don't you take the cattle truck?' suggested Caroline, handing her the keys. 'In fact, why don't you keep it? It's the least we can do to say thank you for your help.'

Ava smiled, showing the gaps in her teeth.

'Don't mind if I do,' she said. 'It's got more room than my caravan!'

'Just don't drive it in the dark,' said Charlie. 'The lights don't work.'

'Oh, don't you worry, my little friend. I don't travel in the dark. It's bad luck, so it is. Move by daylight, party by moonlight, that's my motto!' Ava laughed and blew them a kiss. 'I'll see you again, Charlie Bass!'

Joe and Charlie let Noble Warrior enjoy a pick of grass on the edge of the lane while they waited for the horsebox to arrive. He lifted his head at every strange noise and was still very edgy. Charlie soothed him by running her hand over his body, stroking from the top of his neck towards his shoulder and along his back, down his quarters. She sang to him softly in a low voice and, gradually, he started to relax.

'How did the Chief Inspector know the names of the kidnappers when she arrested them?' asked Larry.

'The police went through the BBC film footage too,' Bill explained. 'They found a really clear shot of their faces. They were both wanted for petty theft and they once tried to steal a pedigree dog, but it bit them and they abandoned it a mile from its home. He found his way back, clever dog. Also Luca Cunningham used to work for Alex Williams. I think, if they ask a few questions, they'll find it was him who stole the rugs and the farm machinery from Cherrydown Stables.'

'So the police might have worked out who took Noddy by themselves,' pondered Joe. 'But they wouldn't have known to look here. The kidnappers would've done serious damage to Noddy if they'd galloped him on that road, and who knows what they'd have done to him afterwards when they found out we couldn't pay the ransom . . .'

Joe's voice drifted off and he shuddered at the thought. Charlie had been thinking the same thing. But their gloomy notions of what might have happened were interrupted by the welcome noise of the Cherrydown Stables horsebox pulling into the field. Noble Warrior whinnied and from the back of the horsebox came an answering neigh.

Nigel, the Cherrydown Head Lad, lowered the side ramp of the horsebox to reveal a palomino head with one blue eye and one brown poking over the partition gate.

'Percy!' cried Charlie. 'They brought you too!'

Charlie climbed into the horsebox to lead Percy

out, but he wasn't going to wait for such niceties. He charged down the ramp, pulling the rope out of Charlie's hands, and made a beeline for Noble Warrior.

'I think he's cross that he's missed out on all the excitement,' Charlie laughed. 'For once, I'll let your bad manners pass, you naughty boy.'

Percy stood nose to nose with Noble Warrior for a moment, but, as soon as he had satisfied himself that his friend was unharmed, he put his head down to wolf as much grass as possible. Noble Warrior visibly relaxed and started to pick grass as well.

'Friends reunited,' smiled Granny Pam. 'Oh, I do LOVE a happy ending!'

Chapter 13

By the time they were on the motorway and heading towards home, it was nearly midnight. Charlie was in the back of the horsebox with Joe so that they could keep an eye on Noble Warrior. In the sleeping area, Harry was lying with a cold towel on his swollen eye, while Larry was snoring loudly. In the front passenger seat, Granny Pam was telling Nigel of her plans to return to the stage soon.

Charlie's parents were following in the car. Charlie poked her head through the hatch that separated the back of the box from the driver's cab.

'How much further?' she asked.

'Not far now,' answered Nigel, as he flicked the indicator to turn off the motorway. 'Half an hour, tops.'

'Tell Joe he can stay in the house tonight,' Granny Pam said to Charlie. 'It's FAR too late for him to go home now.'

Charlie passed on the invitation, but Joe had other ideas.

'Thanks, but I think I'll sleep in the barn,' he said. 'It's not that cold and I'd rather not leave Noddy on his own tonight.'

Percy pushed his nose towards Joe as if to remind him he'd be there too.

'Yes, I know, lad.' Joe patted him playfully. 'But we all know that it only takes a couple of bananas to win your affections, so a fat lot of good you are as a guard horse.'

When they got home, Charlie and Joe put Noble

Warrior and Percy in the barn, with some blankets to keep Joe warm. Then she made her way up to her room, shattered by the day's events.

But, despite her exhaustion, Charlie couldn't sleep. She tossed and turned and looked at her alarm clock every forty minutes. Every time her eyes closed, she had visions of Noble Warrior disappearing again, or saw Polly being thrown to the ground as her pony reared. Boris snuggled into her body, sensing her fear and doing his best to comfort her. Charlie put her arm round him, pulling him tighter. But it was no good. Eventually, she got out of bed and went down to the kitchen. It was still dark outside, but she wasn't the only one up. Her mother stood by the kettle, waiting for it to boil.

'Couldn't you sleep, chicken?' she said.

'I tried,' Charlie replied. 'But I can't stop thinking about what might have happened if we hadn't got to Essex when we did. What if we'd never found Noddy or if they'd hurt him?'

'I know, I know.' Caroline placed a mug of tea in

front of Charlie and sat down beside her. 'But that *didn't* happen and what we've got to try and do is focus on what did, and how we managed, all of us, to get Noble Warrior back. You did an amazing job as team captain, you know.'

'Did I?' Charlie's cheeks flushed red. 'I was so angry all the time. I've never felt like that before and it scared me.'

'That can happen,' her mother replied. 'Lots of things in life will make you angry, but you did well to contain it. I think you've learned so much in the last six months. I don't think even Kate Richardson-Walsh or Steph Houghton would have done better at getting the best out of everyone around them. You stayed calm, you were brilliant at communicating, you reacted quickly and you kept your focus on what you wanted to achieve. It was a fabulous example of T-CUP.'

'Teacup?' asked Charlie, looking down at her chipped mug and wondering what on earth her mother was on about.

'Thinking Clearly Under Pressure,' smiled her

mum. 'It's what Clive Woodward talked about when England won the Rugby World Cup in 2003. He says it's the most important skill you can have in a tense situation and, Charlie, believe me, you've got it.'

Charlie swallowed a mouthful of tea and looked out of the window.

'Mum, will Polly get better?'

Caroline's smile wavered.

'Honestly, darling, I don't know. I spoke to Jasmine this evening to thank her for letting us use the horsebox. She said Polly is stable, but the doctors still don't know what will happen. Her broken leg will mend, but she's got extensive nerve damage. That might get better or it might not. It's possible that she'll be disabled. Only time will tell.'

Charlie furrowed her brow. She wanted so much to help her friend. She wasn't a doctor and she couldn't perform miracles, but there had to be *something* she could do.

The sky was starting to get lighter and she could hear the birds singing. Charlie knew she should go out shortly to check on Joe and the horses.

'Do you want to take a cup of tea to Joe?' said her mother, as if reading her mind.

'Thanks, Mum,' Charlie replied.

Boris led the way as Charlie walked out to the barn with Joe's cup of tea. She found him wrapped in a horse blanket, half sitting, half lying, with his head and upper back resting against Noble Warrior's neck as he lay in the straw.

Percy, ever hopeful of food, got up as Charlie came into the barn, while Noble Warrior flicked his ears and looked at her but didn't try to stand up. Charlie sat down in the straw next to Joe and handed him his tea.

'I think Noddy must have liked you sleeping with him,' she said. 'He's looking much more like his old self.'

Joe stretched his arms.

'He makes a good chair, that's for sure,' he said, sipping the tea gratefully.

'We should talk about Seamus O'Reilly's letter,' Charlie said.

While Noble Warrior was missing, she had almost forgotten about it, but now Noddy was back it was a discussion they needed to have. 'Everyone says he's a really good man. A great trainer too – did you see he won the Irish Derby with Little Lion Man?'

'I know,' replied Joe with a sigh. 'He's amazing.'

'He's got more than two hundred horses at his stables. He'd give you the chance to ride top-class horses all the time,' reasoned Charlie. 'You wouldn't be waiting just for Noddy. He's offering you the chance of a lifetime.'

Joe nodded. 'I know. He says I can go there on trial to see if I like it or not. He'll pay for my travel expenses and give me a decent salary as well.' He paused and looked at Noble Warrior. 'Let's go for a ride. That'll help me decide.'

They rode out slowly into the field where Noble Warrior had gradually learned to gallop, and where he had mastered the art of cantering downhill and round a left corner in preparation for Tattenham Corner at Epsom. Joe was riding with long stirrups, his legs hanging down the sides of Noble Warrior's tummy. He had a light contact on the reins, helping his horse to relax and enjoy himself.

Charlie was trying hard to stop Percy eating grass with every step so she had to keep her reins short.

'I'll give him a trot to check he's sound,' said Joe. 'You stay there and I'll go in a circle round you.'

As he moved forward into trot, Joe shortened his reins slightly and felt the contact with Noble Warrior's mouth. Charlie watched as Noble Warrior arched his neck and lowered his head. His hind legs came right under him as he trotted with power and grace.

'Wow!' she said. 'He looks like a dressage horse.'

Joe started to play with him, asking him to go sideways, to do extended trot, to halt and then rein back. He brought him back to walk and then put his outside leg behind the girth, squeezing him forward into canter. Noble Warrior responded immediately.

'I think he really likes it,' said Joe. 'This is why he was so good at Epsom. He's got natural balance and he's really flexible.'

'Do you think he's got over the kidnapping?' Charlie asked.

'We won't know that until we try him on a racecourse again,' he replied.

'True,' sighed Charlie. 'But I don't want to force him before he's ready. I can't push him to win more races when he's already done us the biggest favour of all. He saved the farm by winning the Derby. Maybe that's where we should leave it and bow out at the top. I know every other trainer would want to go on and win more, but Granny Pam says it's better to be different. She says you should never go with the flow, because the water can get really choppy, what with everyone kicking around you.'

'So we should swim against the current?' asked Joe. 'Sounds like making life harder for yourself, if you ask me.'

'I just don't think we should be greedy,' Charlie replied.

'Well, that's fine,' said Joe. 'But don't confuse greed with ambition. No one ever gets anywhere

207

in sport without wanting to win more. How do you think Andy Murray stays motivated? Or Roger Federer? They've got to the top and now they have to stay there by working with the top coaches and competing against the best players.'

'Exactly.' Charlie reached out to clasp Joe's hand. 'And the best racehorse trainer in the world wants you on his team. You've got to do it. Remember that book Mum gave me before the Derby? *How to Find the Olympian Within*? It says that when you get a choice between stepping out of your comfort zone or staying safe with what you know, you should take the risk and go for the thing that will stretch you. Otherwise you'll never improve.'

'I understand, Charlie, I really do,' said Joe. 'But I've thought about it a lot over the last twenty-four hours. It's hard to explain, but, while Noddy was missing, it felt like I'd lost a part of myself too. I can't leave him and I don't want to leave all of you. I've made my decision. I'm staying here.'

Charlie forced herself to smile. She wasn't sure

Joe was making the right choice, but she did know it was his choice to make.

'Fair enough,' Charlie said. 'But let's take it slowly with Noddy. If he's still OK in a month or two then we can take him to a racecourse and see how he behaves.'

Joe smiled.

'Sounds like a good plan.'

And it *was* a good plan. Over the next month, it became clear that Noble Warrior might not be physically injured, but he was still recovering from his ordeal. One day he would be happy and relaxed and the next he would start sweating for no reason and become agitated. He spooked at any loud noise and a pheasant starting up from the woods would send him galloping halfway across the field.

'Sit tight, Joe!' Charlie shouted, as Noble Warrior flung himself sideways. He started bucking like a bronco. Joe clung on with all his might, his balance and strength tested to the maximum.

'I think he's too fresh,' Joe said, when he had regained control. 'It's been six weeks of gentle exercise now and he's getting bored.'

Noble Warrior flicked his ears, as if listening to the conversation.

Charlie rubbed her chin thoughtfully. Joe was obviously keen to pull on the green-and-gold silks and ride Noble Warrior in a race again. It wasn't easy being a part-time jockey. He wanted and needed to be in the saddle more often, not just watching races on TV.

'OK, let's have a look at the racing calendar,' Charlie said.

The truth was they all needed another challenge. Granny Pam had gone home and Charlie was back at school and struggling to concentrate on her lessons. All she could think about were Noble Warrior and Percy – and her best friend.

Polly's injuries had turned out to be very serious. As well as a broken leg, she had fractured a bone in her lower back and was still in hospital. The doctors said that it would take a long time for her to relearn how to walk – and that she would probably never be able to ride again.

It was devastating news. Charlie visited Polly every day after school, trying to keep her friend positive, but it was clear Polly was having a hard time coming to terms with her disability. Joe visited her with Charlie a couple of times, but, whenever he came, Polly had dried up, seemingly unable to chat in front of him.

'I don't like him seeing me like this,' she'd confided to Charlie. 'I feel so useless and I haven't got anything interesting to say to him. He'll think I'm dull.'

'Rubbish,' said Charlie. 'Joe's really fond of you and he just wants you to get better.' She winked at her best friend. 'And I know you like him too.'

Polly blushed. 'But I get so embarrassed when we talk. He's so talented and confident and I'm ... well, look at me.'

Slowly, though, Polly's mood lifted, and she started to look to the future.

'The physiotherapist says I'm doing really well on my crutches,' she explained one afternoon. 'And the doctors say the cast will come off my leg next week, but I think my parents are worried about me coming home.'

'Why?' asked Charlie.

'They're scared,' answered Polly. 'I can see it in their eyes. They know I'm safe in here, but they don't realize that it's driving me mad. I want to see Munchkin and I want to sleep in my own bed, even if it's hard to get up the stairs.'

Her eyes started to fill up with tears.

'I just want to go home.'

The effort of being brave was draining and Polly had tried really hard. She hadn't complained and she had even eaten the hospital food, despite it tasting of cardboard.

'I know there are lots of people way worse off than me in here,' she said. 'And I play with some of the little kids and chat to the old people who don't get many visitors, but I've had enough now.'

'I don't blame you,' Charlie said. 'I wouldn't last two days in here. I'd miss the animals too much and I'd even miss my brothers, despite them being the most annoying people in the world. Have you talked to your parents about going home?'

Polly sighed. 'Not really. I don't want to pester them and I know they'll say it's up to the doctors.'

'Why don't I try?' suggested Charlie.

Polly reached out for her friend's arm.

'Would you?' she said. 'That'd be brilliant. Mum and Dad love you so much they might just listen.'

'Of course I will,' said Charlie, standing up. 'You just relax and concentrate on getting stronger. I'll see what I can do.'

As Charlie left the hospital, she bumped into Mrs Williams.

'Charlie! Lovely to see you. How is Noble Warrior getting on?' she asked.

'He's on the mend, Mrs Williams, thank you for asking,' answered Charlie. 'But I'm worried he might be bored. He needs a challenge. A bit like

Polly, he's in danger of going backwards if we don't help lead him forwards.'

'A bit like Polly?' said Mrs Williams. 'What do you mean?'

Charlie knew she needed to be careful. If she pushed too hard, Mrs Williams might think she was interfering.

'It's just that there can be a danger in being safe, if you know what I mean.'

'No,' said Mrs Williams with a kindly smile, 'I don't know what you mean. It sounds like you're talking in riddles!'

'I just wonder if Polly needs to go home,' said Charlie simply. 'I'm worried that, staying still, like a pond without plants or fish, she'll go stagnant.'

Mrs Williams laughed. 'Well, you have a very fertile imagination, Charlie Bass, I'll give you that. Mr Williams and I would love to have Polly at home, but we need to make sure she's really ready, you see?'

'I understand completely,' replied Charlie. 'But she needs things too. She needs her own room and her own bed, and she needs to see her pony. Although,' Charlie added thoughtfully, 'if she can't go home to do that, perhaps I can bring Munchkin here . . .'

Mrs Williams looked horrified.

'You can't bring a pony into the hospital! That would be against all sorts of health and safety regulations.'

'When Mary Berry was a little girl, she had polio,' Charlie said. 'She was in hospital for a long, long time and her father knew that she was in danger of getting depressed. So he brought her pony in to see her. It worked wonders.'

Charlie knew that Mrs Williams was a big fan of Mary Berry and that her story might help persuade her of the power of pony love.

'OK,' Mrs Williams laughed. 'You win, Charlie. I'll talk to the doctors today and see what they say. If they don't object, we'll bring Polly home before the week is out. We've made some adjustments to the house to help her get around, but she'll have to adapt to a new way of life.'

'Of course. One step at a time,' smiled Charlie, as she walked away. 'Thanks, Mrs Williams.'

Chapter 14

The year was ticking past and still Charlie and Joe couldn't find the right race for Noble Warrior. The King George VI and Queen Elizabeth Diamond Stakes had been and gone, Goodwood wasn't suitable, York was too far away and even further was Paris, where the Arc de Triomphe was run. That would involve a ferry or a flight and Charlie didn't want to put Noble Warrior through a traumatic journey. So they waited. Joe continued to milk the cows in the morning and then ride Noble Warrior in the fields around Folly Farm. He even took him over to Cherrydown Stables to work alongside Alex Williams's best racehorses.

The first journey in the new horsebox proved tricky. Noble Warrior had reluctantly followed Percy up the ramp, but wouldn't settle, hopping from one foot to the other and weaving his head from side to side for the whole journey. He was dripping with sweat by the time they arrived and they had to wash him down before he was tacked up.

Joe followed Alex Williams's immaculately turned out racehorses up the path to the top of the Downs. He shortened his stirrups and prepared Noble Warrior for his gallop. They would go at a sensible, even pace for the first five furlongs and then quicken up and finish off as fast as Noble Warrior could go. Charlie had perfected the art of cutting the corners on the gallops so that Noddy never realized he was galloping without Percy.

'He's still got it,' said Alex Williams, clicking his

stopwatch as Noddy hurtled across the finish. 'Extraordinary!'

Polly stood alongside him on her crutches. The full extent of her injuries was clear now and the doctors knew she would never fully recover. She had lost the feeling in her left leg and, when she tried to compensate with the right, it put her in a lot of discomfort. Charlie could see Polly occasionally wince with pain and she thought her friend was incredibly brave.

Polly and Charlie had tried to persuade her parents to let her try riding Munchkin, but they wouldn't agree, much to Polly's frustration. She said Charlie was the only person who didn't treat her as if she had 'fragile' stickers all over her. Charlie didn't think she was doing anything special; she just looked for what Polly *could* do and let her get on with it.

However, the anger Charlie felt towards Noble Warrior's kidnappers every time she looked at Polly was not going away. They had no idea how much damage they had caused with their thoughtlessness that day. If Polly could never ride again, it was all their fault. And sometimes, Charlie felt, her fault too, because, if she had been at home that night, Noble Warrior might not have been kidnapped.

But Charlie tried to stop herself thinking too much about the 'what ifs' and 'maybes'. There was no point. She couldn't change what had happened in the past, she could only influence what might happen next. At least the kidnappers were safely behind bars and could no longer hurt anyone.

'What do you think, Polly?' asked Charlie, as Noble Warrior raced past.

'I reckon he'll be spot on with another couple of gallops,' she replied. 'By the way, I was looking at Dad's racing calendar and there's a race on Champions Day at Ascot that might suit him. It's a mile and a quarter, so a bit shorter than the Derby, but I looked at the racecourse map and I reckon you and Percy could just about get beyond the winning post before Noble Warrior reaches it, but you'd better not hang about!'

'That sounds perfect, Polly. Thanks a million.'

Charlie saw her friend beaming in delight and realized again how important it was to make the people she loved and trusted feel part of the team. 'Then that's what we'll aim for. It makes sense that he should race on Champions Day because that's what he is. He's our champion.'

Charlie told Joe the plan as they were walking back from their morning exercise the next day. The horses were flicking away flies with their tails and had settled into an easy rhythm. Noble Warrior was more laid back now he was getting extra exercise and had more to think about.

'It's a great plan, Charlie,' said Joe. 'I can't wait!'

Maybe everything will work out for the best, thought Charlie. *Joe will be happy, Noble Warrior will prove himself a champion and Polly can take some of the credit.*

Once word got out that Noble Warrior was going to return to a racecourse, the media went into a frenzy.

The BBC documentary about how the racehorse who wouldn't gallop became a Derby winner had been updated to include the story of his kidnapping. It was shown on television in July, a week after his ordeal. Millions of people had watched it, but no one had seen Noble Warrior or Charlie since then. Now the racehorse who disappeared was about to reappear. And the phone wouldn't stop ringing.

'I'm not giving interviews,' Charlie said for the hundredth time, through gritted teeth.

'But it's good for racing,' Harry argued.

'And it's the ultimate feel-good story,' Larry added. 'Shergar was never found, but Noble Warrior was – and now he's going to make a triumphant return.'

'You don't know that,' Charlie snapped. 'No one knows if he's going to win. He's a horse, not a machine.'

'She's right not to build up people's expectations,' Joe explained. 'I'm feeling nervous enough about riding at Ascot for the first time. I don't need any more pressure.'

'Pressure is a privilege!' shouted Harry and Larry together. 'That's what they say.'

'Well, it's not feeling like a privilege right now,' said Joe. 'In fact, it's making me feel a bit sick.'

On the day of the race, Polly joined Charlie in the back of the horsebox with Noble Warrior as they made their way to Ascot. Percy, of course, was alongside him too and he looked pleased to have an outing.

'He's missed the attention far more than Noddy has,' observed Charlie, offering him an apple so that he could bite half of it. She had intended to give the other half to Noble Warrior, but Percy had other ideas.

'Oi!' But it was too late. Percy had grabbed the whole apple and it was firmly in his mouth, showing through his cheeks as he crunched it into smaller pieces. 'You were meant to share that! You're a greedy, selfish little monster!'

Charlie laughed as she stroked his face and he put his ears back at her.

'I really don't understand why Noddy loves you so much. Millions wouldn't.'

'They say opposites attract and maybe that's true for horses as well,' said Polly. 'The weird thing is, the more relaxed and confident Noddy gets, the more miserable Percy becomes.'

Charlie nodded. 'He doesn't like sharing the limelight, but I do hope Noddy puts his best foot forward. I want Joe to shine. I don't want him to regret turning down the chance to work with Seamus O'Reilly.'

'Well, I'm glad he didn't go,' Polly said before she could stop herself.

Charlie bashed her on the arm playfully.

'I know you are,' she teased.

Polly blushed. 'Well, he is cute, you have to admit.'

'Polly!' exclaimed Charlie. 'Stop it! He's like part of my family! He's the big brother that doesn't let me down and doesn't annoy me.'

Bill Bass parked the horsebox outside the stables, which were far away from the noise and colour of the racecourse. Caroline, Harry and Larry spilled out and disappeared to sign the papers that would allow them security clearance into the area where all the day's runners were stabled.

They had been asked if Noddy would join in the Parade of Champions before the first race started, but Charlie had refused. Despite Noble Warrior's improved temperament, she knew there was still a chance of him getting spooked by a big crowd. She didn't want him distracted or excited before his big race. When the time came, they would lead him up the hill, past the hospital and over the road. Only then would he recognize that he was back on a racecourse.

Once they were in the stables, Polly leaned on one crutch and helped Charlie brush Noble Warrior. Then she stood by his head and handed Charlie elastic bands as she plaited his mane.

'They're sending a buggy to take you and my parents up the hill,' explained Charlie. 'I'll meet you in the paddock.'

Polly nodded.

As Charlie put the final touches to the plait in Noble Warrior's forelock, Polly leaned forward to kiss him on the nose. 'You be a good boy today and we can show the world that you're not a one-race wonder.'

'He likes having you around, Polly,' Charlie said, as she stroked Noble Warrior. 'He always seems better behaved when you're here.'

'Maybe he recognizes another damaged soul,' Polly said thoughtfully.

'You're not damaged,' Charlie retorted. 'You're just different and so is he. But perhaps he knows you know how he feels. It's a sort of kinship. Maybe you should ride him one day.'

Polly laughed. 'Yeah, like that's going to happen! My parents won't even let me get on my own pony. I can't see them letting me ride a highly strung racehorse who only Joe Butler can control. You do have some weird ideas, Charlie!'

'I'm just saying I think you two get along very well. That's all.'

'You won't *believe* what I've just found out,' said Harry, walking into the stable with Larry trailing in his wake.

'Hmm,' Charlie said sarcastically. 'That you're not the sun, and the earth doesn't revolve around you?'

Harry ignored her.

'Seamus O'Reilly's travelling Head Lad told me that Joe turned down the chance to work there. No one in the yard could believe it. Mr O'Reilly was really upset. All the other trainers know about it too and think it shows a lack of ambition. That's why Polly's dad is the only one who's giving him any rides.'

'Poor Joe,' said Polly. 'That doesn't seem very fair. It's hardly a crime to turn down a job.'

'It's my fault,' said Charlie. 'I was banging on about not doing what everyone else would do, about being unique and not being greedy. I was talking about Noble Warrior, but Joe must have thought I was talking about the job with O'Reilly. I think that's why he didn't take it.'

Caroline appeared at the stable door just in time to hear the end of the conversation.

'That's not true,' she said firmly. 'He didn't take it because he prefers to be on the farm with all of us and he wanted the chance to ride Noble Warrior in a race again. You saw how he was this morning, like a little kid on Christmas Eve. It's the most excited he's been for months. He loves Noddy and he hates that the press have said the Derby was a fluke. He wants to prove them wrong.'

Charlie nodded. Her mother was making sense, but she hoped he hadn't made a huge mistake. She needed Noble Warrior to make it worth his while.

'We haven't got long until the race. Can you guys just give me a hand with Percy?' she asked her brothers.

Harry and Larry swung into action, each grabbing a brush. Charlie buttoned up her smart jacket as she watched her brothers work. They weren't all bad: they just didn't think about what they could do to help. They always had to be asked.

Percy looked furious at the indignity of being

speed-groomed, but his attitude changed as he walked up the hill with Charlie in the saddle, leading Noble Warrior towards the parade ring. He pricked his ears at the sound of the crowd and strutted along proudly. Charlie patted him on the neck.

'I know. Finally, the attention you deserve. Your adoring audience awaits.'

Harry and Larry led Noble Warrior behind, one on each side, as they had seen Seamus O'Reilly's staff do with their best horses.

As they entered the paddock, Charlie realized that her assumption that it wouldn't be as busy as Derby Day was wide of the mark. There were people crammed up against the white fence and thousands more on the steps all around, as well as people standing on balconies reaching up into the sky. She had never seen a grandstand so enormous. Apart from the Union flags fluttering from its sides, it looked like a giant spaceship that had landed from a planet far away.

Everywhere Charlie looked there were people

in cheerfully coloured outfits. She spotted the Queen in a bright green jacket and matching hat. Charlie swallowed. This was going to be harder than she'd thought. She tried to calm her nerves and looked behind to check on Noble Warrior as they made their way under the tunnel and into the brightness of the paddock.

Percy started to jig-jog and the motion must have woken up his digestive system because, as he turned left to lead Noble Warrior in a clockwise circle, his bottom started to produce the familiar trumpet solo that seemed to accompany his every major appearance in public. Charlie tried to smile, but her face went red so fast that she looked like a traffic light.

'I'm so sorry,' she said to the crowd at the front rail. 'He does this when he's nervous.'

The bottom-burp serenade lasted all the way past the weighing room, beyond the TV studio and right over to the other side. Charlie didn't know where to look and she could hear the crowd giggling. She glanced to the inside of the paddock and saw the Queen was also laughing. As Charlie caught her eye, the Queen waved a white-gloved hand at her and smiled.

Oh, well, Charlie thought. *At least we're memorable . . .*

Behind her, Noble Warrior was also taking in the scene. He had seemed happy enough to follow Percy, but, when Charlie looked round again, she noticed he had started to sweat on the side of his neck. She was suddenly aware of how loud the public address system was, as the announcer turned his attention to them.

'And finally, Your Majesty, my lords, ladies and gentlemen, we come to the star of the day.' The man's voice boomed from the speakers. 'Led by his trainer, Charlie Bass, riding Percy the pony, it's this year's record-breaking Derby winner, the racehorse who was kidnapped and then found, and who makes his reappearance on a racecourse for the first time in four months: NOBLE WARRIOR!'

As the announcer shouted his name, the crowd erupted into cheering. Noble Warrior suddenly stopped and reared up in fear. Harry let go of his lead rope, but Larry, clinging on for dear life, was swung up into the air.

Charlie turned Percy round and tried to calm Noble Warrior.

'Steady, boy! It's all right. They're just pleased to see you. Well done, Larry, for keeping hold of him.'

Harry grabbed his rope back and both of them started stroking Noble Warrior's neck. His eyes were still bulging and he was a coiled spring of nervous energy, but he seemed to be back in control of himself.

Then, on the road outside the racecourse, Charlie heard the blowing of a bugle. She had no idea that it was a tradition at Ascot for some racegoers to arrive by horse-drawn carriage. One party had clearly timed their arrival to coincide with the start of the big race and a huge carriage with two large black horses was making its way down the high street. Charlie could hear the rattling of the wheels on the road and the sound of the carriage driver urging the horses to keep up the pace of their trot.

She was not the only one who heard it.

The sight and sound of the carriage was the spark that lit the bonfire in Noble Warrior's head. For all the calming work Charlie and Joe had done with him at home, the trauma of the kidnapping was still with him. He had been taken in the middle of the night from the only place he felt safe, separated from his best friend by two men who abused him. The whole episode may have lasted less than twenty-four hours, but, Charlie realized, it might take Noddy a lifetime to get over it.

She didn't have any time to consider the long-term implications because, right here and now, she needed to make sure he didn't hurt anyone. In a split second, Noddy had reared again and shaken himself free of his lead ropes. He shot off at top speed with the wild look of old about him. His tail was up in the air, his nostrils were flared and the whites of his eyes betrayed his terror. The people in the middle of the paddock scattered, running for the area reserved for the prize-giving, where they knew they couldn't be trampled or kicked. Cameras clicked as the photographers zoomed in for a shot of the crazy racehorse who suddenly *wanted* to gallop. The crowd gasped as he bucked and kicked and reared and snorted.

Bill and Caroline fanned out to try to catch him,

Harry and Larry scampered round the edge of the paddock, while Joe came running out of the weighing room. If the paddock was a clock face, they tried to cover every hour.

But one person refused to seek cover. Unable to move fast enough to get out of danger, Polly leaned on her crutches and stood her ground.

'Polly! Polly, get out of the way!' Jasmine Williams screamed from behind the paddock rails. 'Somebody, get my daughter out of there!'

Noble Warrior was like a dragon breathing fire. He whinnied and pranced in the centre of the paddock, suddenly breaking into a gallop and then skidding to a halt. He slid past Bill and Caroline, changed direction as he got near Harry, avoided Joe and Charlie and gave Larry the slip.

'Steady, boy. Just steady up.'

Noble Warrior's ears flickered backwards and forwards at the sound of the calm voice. He started to slow down. He looked warily to all sides. He was breathing heavily, but slowly his tail lowered and he looked towards the person who was speaking.

'That's it,' said Polly. 'Just calm down now.'

Noble Warrior started to walk forward, his head bowed.

'That's a good boy. Let's just pretend this didn't happen. There we are.'

'No!' Jasmine Williams whimpered. 'He'll knock her over! Somebody, please save her!'

Charlie looked towards Mrs Williams and caught her eye, trying to calm her too. She knew no one could interfere at this point. If anyone ran towards Noble Warrior, he might take off again. Charlie put her hands out to the others, warning them to stay back. This would have to play out slowly, without Noddy feeling threatened in any way.

Polly seemed to be the only person who wasn't frightened. She smiled at Noble Warrior as he walked towards her, still snorting and flicking his ears. She kept speaking in an even tone, never raising or quickening her voice.

'There's a good fella, that's it. Slowly does it. Good boy.'

She gently lowered one crutch to the ground to

give her a free hand and, as Noble Warrior reached his head towards her, she lifted her hand to stroke his face, before very delicately taking hold of the lead rope that was dangling down from his headcollar. She leaned against him for support and he seemed to know that he must now behave.

'That was *amazing*.' Joe appeared by Polly's side and retrieved her crutch from the ground. 'I thought I had a knack with difficult horses and, to be honest, I thought I knew Noddy, but that was in a different league.'

Charlie walked slowly towards them on Percy, who whinnied. Noble Warrior nudged him with his nose. His sides were heaving and he seemed exhausted, all the fight in him gone.

'We'd better get out of here before we cause any more trouble,' Charlie said. 'Joe, we can't possibly run him now. I'm so sorry. I know how much you were looking forward to it.'

'Oh, don't worry about me,' he said bravely. 'I've only ever wanted to do what's right for

Noddy. If he doesn't want to be a racehorse any more then I don't want to be a jockey.'

'Well, I think that would be a shame,' said Polly, looking Joe full in the eye. She didn't stammer or hesitate or blush. Still leaning on Noble Warrior's shoulder for support, she had the confidence to say what she wanted to. 'You were born to be a jockey. *You* should be in that winner's enclosure, even if Noddy doesn't want to be.'

This time, Joe was the one whose cheeks coloured.

'Thanks, Polly. I appreciate that.'

'She's right, Joe,' added Charlie. 'You shouldn't let us hold you back. Seamus O'Reilly has got two runners in this race, so why don't you try to have a word with him afterwards?'

Joe took a deep breath and sighed.

'You're right. I will. I'll see you in a bit.' With a smile, he headed off towards the weighing room.

'Come on, let's get Noddy back to the stables.' Charlie gave Percy a squeeze to lead the way. 'Polly, you'd better find your mother. I don't think she's best pleased with me. We'll catch up later.'

Harry and Larry led Noble Warrior away. He had calmed down now and was happy to follow Percy. It was almost as if nothing had happened, but Charlie knew that everything had changed. Noble Warrior couldn't be a racehorse any more, not if he was going to be scared by huge crowds and loud noises. They would have to come up with something else for him to do.

But that was a problem for another day. Right now, Charlie just wanted to get him home.

Epilogue

The next day, Noddy and Percy were turned out into the field at Folly Farm to have a pick of grass. Charlie and Polly leaned on the fence and watched them grazing happily, while Boris barked at a magpie that had the cheek to perch nearby.

'How can he be so different from one day to the next?' Charlie mused out loud.

'Like you said, he's a horse not a machine,' Polly

replied. 'He was already scared and the sight of that carriage finished him off. It must've brought back terrible memories and he thought he was going to be hurt again. I know what he feels like.'

'But you stayed so calm. Weren't you frightened he might knock you down?' Charlie asked.

'No, I wasn't. Honestly, I know it sounds crazy, but it never crossed my mind. I sort of trust him not to hurt me. I'm not sure I know why, but I do.'

'Well, I guess we'll have to find something for him to do that doesn't have any bad associations in his head,' said Charlie. 'I've been thinking about what you said about horses learning new skills, like polo or horseball. And I've been reading about an organization that helps with that called Retraining of Racehorses.'

'Sounds good,' said Polly. 'There's got to be something else that will suit him.'

'Maybe it'll be something that will suit you too,' suggested Charlie. 'He obviously loves you and someone has to ride him.'

Polly looked thoughtful.

'Why don't you want to ride him?' she asked.

'Oh, Percy would never get over it if I deserted him,' Charlie laughed. 'Besides, I think you and Noddy might be able to help each other. I quite like being the trainer, if I'm honest, so it might be the best solution for all of us.'

They looked again into the field. Noddy was rolling around, as he loved to do, scratching his back on the grass. He squealed as he got to his feet and trotted off to join Percy, who never lifted his head from the serious job of eating as much grass as he could.

'Did Joe talk to Seamus O'Reilly?' Polly asked.

'Yes, I did.' Joe appeared behind them. He was wearing jeans and a jacket and in his hand was a soft duffel bag. 'He said he totally understood why I'd turned him down and he respected my loyalty to everyone here.' Joe gestured to Noble Warrior in the field and to the whole farm.

'In fact, he said that he admired my decision because it wasn't what most people would have done. But I guess Noddy helped me change my mind. You did too, Polly.'

Polly smiled but didn't look away.

'It was what you said about being in that winner's enclosure,' Joe explained. 'I suddenly understood that, if I played it safe, I'd never know if I could only ride one horse or whether I could really make it as a jockey. I don't want to always wonder what might have been.'

'So you're going?' asked Polly.

Joe lifted his bag on to his shoulder.

'Yes. It's not forever and Mr O'Reilly says I can come back whenever I need to. And I hope I'll see you at the races occasionally.'

'Of course you will!' Charlie exclaimed. 'Just you try to keep us away.'

'I'm so excited for you,' Polly said. 'You'll get the chance to ride in all the big races and everyone will see how good a jockey you are. You'll be so famous that you won't even bother talking to the likes of us.'

'Oh, I don't think that will happen,' Joe

countered. 'I'll always have time for you two.'

'We'll miss you, Joe,' Charlie said. 'But I promise that Polly and I will look after Noble Warrior for you.'

Joe smiled. 'I don't doubt it for a second. Now, let's say goodbye properly because I've got a plane to catch.'

Joe put his arms round both girls and squeezed them tight. Boris jumped up to try to join in the family hug.

'It's a new beginning for all of us,' Charlie said. 'Good luck, Joe.'

'And good luck to you two. Polly, I heard what Charlie suggested and she's right – you should ride Noddy. He'd be good for you. And Charlie, you just keep being the person you are. You've got a gift, you know – a very special knack of knowing how to make other people tick. You're one in a million, Charlie Bass.'

As the sun dipped in the sky, turning it a rosy shade of pink, Charlie thought Joe's eyes looked a little watery and his bottom lip was quivering as he turned to walk away.

Boris barked, Noble Warrior whinnied and Percy, true to form, farted a farewell.

Join CHARLIE on more adventures!

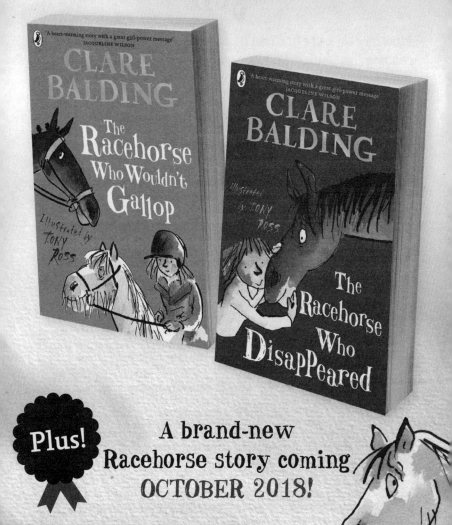

'A heart-warming story with a great girl-power message'
JACQUELINE WILSON

CLARE BALDING

THE Racehorse Who Wouldn't Gallop

Illustrated by TONY ROSS

'A heart-warming story with a great girl-power message'
JACQUELINE WILSON

CLARE BALDING

Illustrated by TONY ROSS

THE Racehorse Who DisapPeared

Plus! A brand-new Racehorse story coming OCTOBER 2018!

TEST YOUR KNOWLEDGE!

Quiz

How closely were you paying attention when you were reading this book? Take our quiz to find out! But beware – the questions start off easy but get quite tricky at the end!

> Tip! Write your answers in pencil so the pen doesn't show through the page!

Q1. What is the name of Charlie's best friend?

....

Q2. What is the name of the TV show Larry and Harry want to create?

....

Q3. What did Charlie's mum put in her gingerbread cake instead of carrots?

....

Q4. Where does the champion trainer Seamus O'Reilly want Joe to move to?

....

Q5. What fruit does Percy love?

....

Q6. Who does BBC Breakfast want to interview about Noble Warrior?

....

Q7. How was Percy poisoned by the kidnappers?

....

Q8. How much was Noble Warrior worth when Charlie bought him?

....

Q9. How much money do the kidnappers want in return for Noble Warrior?

....

Q10. Why do the two police officers have the same surname?

....

Q11. What spooked Munchkin the pony, causing Polly's accident?

....

Q12. What badge was on the kidnapper's baseball cap?

....

Q13. What do the kidnappers plan to do with Noble Warrior if they can't get the ransom money?

....

Q14. What is the name of Charlie's fortune-teller friend?

....

Q15. What is T-CUP?

....

Q16. What book did Charlie's mum give her before the Derby?

....

Q17. What devastating news does Polly receive?

....

Q18. What is the name of the day at Ascot when Noble Warrior races again?

....

Q19. Who waves at Charlie when the crowd are laughing at Noble Warrior's 'bottom-burp'?

....

Q20. What scares Noble Warrior, making him unable to race?

....

Now turn over the page to see how many you got right!

The Racehorse Who Disappeared – Answers!

Check your answers to the quiz below. How did you do?

1. Polly
2. *Strictly Come Chicken Dancing*
3. Mashed potato
4. Ireland
5. Bananas
6. Charlie, Caroline, Bill and Joe
7. Tranquillizer injected into six bananas
8. A thousand pounds
9. A million pounds
10. They are brother and sister
11. A truck driving too fast

12. Essex Eagles
13. Race him illegally to win money
14. Ava
15. Thinking Clearly Under Pressure
16. *How to Find the Olympian Within*
17. That she might never fully recover nor be able to ride again
18. Champions Day
19. The Queen
20. A carriage

15–20 correct:	Astounding! You are a true champion – first place!
10–14 correct:	Well done! You were just pipped to the post, but you're still in second place!
5–9 correct:	Not too bad. It's a third-place rosette for you – better luck next time!
1–4 correct:	Oh dear. You may need to go back and read the story again to brush up on your know-how!

Author Q & A

Puffin met up with author Clare Balding to ask her some nosy questions. Here's what she had to say ...

Q. Why did you decide to write about horses?

A. I grew up surrounded by horses (my father was a racehorse trainer) so it seemed a good idea to stick to something I knew well! Also I love horses and I think they can bring out the best in us as human beings.

Q. Were you like Charlie when you were growing up?

A. I was much naughtier, but I can certainly identify with being the outsider at school and with having 'powerful legs'! Also I loved trying to coax difficult ponies or horses to better behaviour and to try to help them fulfil their potential.

Q. Did you base Harry and Larry on people you know? They seem pretty awful!

A. I have two nephews and a niece whose age gaps are similar, but Jonno and Toby aren't nearly as badly behaved as Harry and Larry, although they find them very funny characters. Flora, who is five, was the inspiration for Charlie.

Q. You've written books for adults before, but *The Racehorse Who Wouldn't Gallop* was your first book for children. Was it easy to write this book, or hard?

A. The story was in my head, but making sure the plot worked, developing the characters and keeping it moving all took a lot of work. I rewrote nearly all of it and took out or added sections as I went along. Writing fiction is fun, but it is a challenge!

Q. How long does it take to write a book?

A. It does depend on how easily the creative juices are flowing and some chapters or episodes (such as the fortune-teller scene at Epsom) come really naturally and fast. The hardest part is starting and I find the first chapter the most difficult. I then try to give myself a month of regular writing (every day if possible) to get the bulk of the plot and characterization worked out.

Q. Is it really possible to ride a cow, like Charlie does?

A. Yes, but it wouldn't be very comfortable and they wouldn't be able to carry heavy weights as horses do. I based that on what the former champion jockey Kieren Fallon told me. He didn't ride a horse until he was eighteen, but he jumped on plenty of cows when he was young.

Q. What would be your one piece of advice for someone just starting out who wants to ride or train professionally?

A. Go to a trainer in your school holidays and definitely go to the British Racing School (as Joe does in the book). My father and my brother have had many young boys and girls at their stables who have never ridden before and end up riding in races. One of them even won the Derby.

Q. What is your favourite racecourse and why?

A. I love Ascot for its size and grandeur, and I enjoy Goodwood for its landscape and relative intimacy, but for jump racing nothing beats Cheltenham!

Q. Will you be writing more books? If so, what will they be about?

A. Definitely. I will see what adventures Charlie might have next as I think her patience with animals and her problem-solving skills could be useful in other arenas.

Q. You present on so many different sports all around the world. Do you have a favourite place and a favourite sporting event?

A. London 2012 was the ultimate highlight, and to work on the Olympics and Paralympics in my home city will never be topped. I love the big multi-sport events and have enjoyed various Winter Olympics and Commonwealth Games as well, but of course I love anything with horses – racing, eventing, show jumping and dressage are all wonderful to cover.

Thanks for answering our questions, Clare!

Fantastic Facts!

Read these facts about ponies and horses. How many did you already know?

- There are more than two hundred breeds of ponies, but the Shetland Pony is the best-known.

- When compared to standard-sized horses, ponies are actually stronger, pound for pound.

- During the Industrial Revolution, some ponies were called 'pit ponies' as they were used to haul coal.

- Ponies and horses have two blind spots where they cannot see. One blind spot is behind them and if they sense someone or something behind them, they will give a powerful kick.

- In the wild, ponies often live in harsh, bleak areas such as moors and fields, where they are able to survive with little food.

- All members of the horse family have just one toe (a hoof) on each foot. For this reason they are often called 'odd-toed animals'.

- Stallions (male horses) defend their territory and protect their mares (female horses) by lashing out with their front feet.

- Horses have the largest eyes of any land mammal.

- A baby horse of one year or younger is called a foal.

- Horse-riding is often used as a form of therapy for people with disabilities.

- Horses can sleep both lying down and standing up.

- Horses usually gallop at around 27 mph but the fastest recorded sprinting speed of a horse was 55 mph!

- Estimates suggest that there are around 60 million horses in the world.

- About an hour after a foal is born, it can stand up, and within a few hours it is able to trot along by its mother.

- The scientific name for a horse is *Equus ferus caballus*.

- Horses have excellent senses, including good hearing, eyesight and a tremendous sense of balance.

Pony Grooming - Top Tips!

Here are some inside tips to get your pony (or horse!) looking fit for a meeting with the Queen!

Treat the feet!

Take a good look at your pony's hooves when you pick them out. Does he need a supplement to help with horn growth? Could he benefit from some luxurious hoof grease? Give your pony's hooves a good wash so you can really see what you've got down there, then treat the feet!

Marvellous manes

Give manes some TLC. Use a detangling spray to make manes more manageable, and then transform your pony's mop into his crowning glory by using a gorgeous conditioner or mane shine! Keep manes looking good by only ever using your fingers or a body brush – never a plastic curry comb, which splits the hair!

Head to tail

A face brush works well on your pony's head – or, even better, rinse an old towel in some hot water, wring it out and give your pony a hot-towel face wash! Ponies love it and it brings up the shine!

Body beautiful

A rubber curry comb, used in a circular motion, is fantastic at bringing up all the dead hair out of the coat. Once you've been all over your pony in this way, brush with your body brush and then try the hot towel treatment, as described for his face, all over to get rid of any leftover dust and grease. Do this every day for a week and you'll really see a transformation. A spray conditioner can then do its job!

The tail-end

Detangle the clean tail with a spray, brush with a body brush and use conditioner to make it look gorgeous.

Bath time

Wait for a warm, sunny day then use a proper horse shampoo, rinse him well afterwards and make sure he doesn't get cold as he dries off.

Insider top tip!

If your pony gets dusty, simply dunk your metal curry comb in a bucket of warm water, shake off and run your body brush over it before using on your pony. Repeat this every four or five strokes, and you'll see the dust disappear. This is great for ponies growing out their clip – try it and see!

Tools of the trade!

Body brush – removes grease from the coat – use with hot water to get rid of dust

Hoof pick – lets you see the condition of the hooves

Dandy brush – removes dried mud from ponies and dead hair from the inside of rugs!

Face brush – soft brush for use on the face

Rubber curry comb – perfect for getting rid of your pony's old, dead winter coat

Sweat scraper – to remove water after a bath

Metal curry comb – used to clean the body brush – NOT for use on your pony!

Plastic curry comb – removes mud and moulting hair

Flick brush – flicks dirt off your pony

Do you like listening to stories?

Listen to Charlie Bass's adventures on AUDIOBOOK!

Read by Clare Balding

Scan the QR code to listen to an extract.

WHAT'S YOUR PERFECT PONY BREED?

Choosing the right breed is an essential part of finding your perfect match. Take the quiz to find the one for you

1. What personality trait are you attracted to the most?

- Strong-minded
- Kind
- Relaxed
- Cheeky

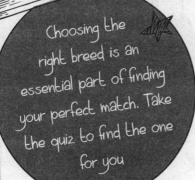

2. What's your fave pony-related activity?

- Hacking
- Jumping
- Cuddles
- Plaiting manes and tails

3. What's your fave colour of pony?

- Brown
- Black
- Chestnut
- Grey

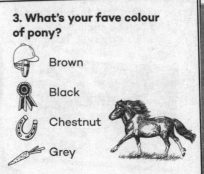

4. What's your ideal pony size?

- 14hh – for the big jumps
- 12hh – nice and low to the ground
- 9hh – perfect squeezing size
- 13.2hh – nice and chunky

5. What new discipline would you most like to try?

- Driving
- Anything and everything
- Showing
- Racing

Turn over for your perfect match!

MOSTLY

You matched with the super-cute **Shetland** pony! They know their own minds and can be stubborn, but are the perfect size for cuddling and can be the ultimate BFF.

MOSTLY

You've chosen the same as the Queen! Known for being her fave breed, **Fell** ponies are very kind but also hardy, so can cope with almost anything. They often have long manes, too, perfect for plaiting!

MOSTLY

Strong choice! **Connemaras** can turn their hooves to anything – you name it, they ace it! They're also super-intelligent and are well known for having great temperaments.

MOSTLY

Exmoor ponies are small in stature but super-strong, have big hearts and a good sense of humour. You'll be the envy of all your mates because they're mega cute, too!

This quiz is from PONY magazine, which is available every four weeks from all good newsagents.

5 WAYS TO MAKE YOUR PONY LOVE YOU

We all want our fave ponies to love us, but can we really make it happen?! Yes, is the answer! Here's how

Gain his trust
Trust is key to having a good bond with your pony. Taking the time to understand your pony's behaviour and learning how to react appropriately to it will help him gain trust in you.

Give him what he needs
Ponies need the 'three Fs' – friends, freedom and forage – to survive. Make sure your fave pony has everything he needs to be healthy and you'll be off to a great start!

Respect his space
We all love pony cuddles and most ponies appreciate the extra attention, too. But it's still important to let him chill out in his field or stable for a rest after you've ridden.

Keep things fun
Make sure you keep his riding routine varied. Include a mixture of flatwork, hacking and jumping, as well as riding alone and with your friends, so neither of you ever get bored!

Spend quality time together
Rather than only getting him in to ride, spend some quality time with your pony – before long you'll know him inside-out and back-to-front!

These tips are from PONY magazine, which is available every four weeks from all good newsagents.